"This farmer is never going to take another wife."

Coralie was shocked. "Do you really want to spend the rest of your life alone?" she asked him. "Your daughters are growing up fast. They won't be living at home for many more years."

"I'll worry about that when the time comes. Until then I'm a confirmed bachelor."

"But don't you miss having a...a..."

She stumbled over the term, but Jim said it for her. "A bed partner? Damn right I do. I didn't say I never get lonely." He chuckled. "But take it from me, lust is not a good enough basis for a marriage. It doesn't last, and when it's cooled off there's nothing left to bind a man and woman together except obligation, and that can be a trap."

It sounded to her as if that trap had closed off his heart and taken it prisoner. What a shame, because he had so much to give a woman.

Dear Reader,

Happy Valentine's Day! Your response to our FABULOUS FATHERS has been tremendous, so our very special valentine to you is the start of our SUPER FABULOUS FATHERS—larger-than-life super dads who make super husbands! And Barbara McMahon's *Sheik Daddy* is just that. Years ago, gorgeous Ben Shalik had loved Megan O'Sullivan with all his heart, then disappeared, leaving her with a baby girl he never knew existed. And now, the royal daddy was back.... Look for more SUPER FABULOUS FATHERS throughout the year.

To celebrate the most romantic day of the year all month long, we're proud to present VALENTINE BRIDES. Reader favorite, author Phyllis Halldorson starts off the series with *Mail Order Wife*, which is exactly what confirmed bachelor Jim Buckley finds waiting on his doorstep! Christine Scott's *Cinderella Bride* proves that fairy tales can come true when Cynthia Gilbert reluctantly says "I do" to a marriage of convenience. In *The Husband Hunt* by Linda Lewis, Sarah Brannan's after a groom, but the man she's in love with proposes to be something *entirely* different.

You won't want to miss our other VALENTINE BRIDES—*Make-Believe Mom* by Elizabeth Sites and *Going to the Chapel* by Alice Sharpe. Because when Cupid strikes—marriage is sure to follow!

Happy Reading!

Melissa Senate
Senior Editor

Please address questions and book requests to:
Silhouette Reader Service
U.S.: 3010 Walden Ave., P.O. Box 1325, Buffalo, NY 14269
Canadian: P.O. Box 609, Fort Erie, Ont. L2A 5X3

MAIL ORDER WIFE
Phyllis Halldorson

Silhouette
ROMANCE™
Published by Silhouette Books
America's Publisher of Contemporary Romance

SILHOUETTE BOOKS

ISBN 0-373-19133-2

MAIL ORDER WIFE

Copyright © 1996 by Phyllis Halldorson

Printed in U.S.A.

Books by Phyllis Halldorson

PHYLLIS HALLDORSON

met her real-life Prince Charming at age sixteen. She married him a year later, and they settled down to raise a family. A compulsive reader, Phyllis dreamed of someday finding the time to write stories of her own. That time came when her two youngest children reached adolescence. When she was introduced to romance novels, she knew she had found her long-delayed vocation. After all, how could she write anything else after living all those years with her very own Silhouette hero?

Dear Reader,

February 14th is a very special day for my husband and me. It was on that day quite a few years ago that our first son was born. Our most memorable Valentine, one that can never be topped and grows even dearer with each passing year.

Happy Birthday, Gerry!

Happy Valentine's Day,

Phyllis Halldorson

Chapter One

James Buckley paused halfway up the steps to the wraparound porch of the weathered old Buckley family farmhouse and glared at his father. "What do you mean Mrs. Winters quit?" he howled. "She hasn't even been here long enough to clean up the mess the last housekeeper left."

"That seems to be part of the trouble," Amos Buckley, better known as Buck, said as he mopped at his cold windburned face with the blue bandanna he kept partially tucked into the hip pocket of his worn jeans. "Guess she had a row with the girls this morning. She said the place is a pigsty and she can't keep it clean because they throw their stuff everywhere and never pick anything up. When I got back from town about eleven o'clock she had her clothes packed and was just waitin' for one of us to show up so she could collect what money was due her before she left."

There was no condemnation in Buck's tone, but Jim winced, anyway. He didn't need his father to point out to him that he was too lenient with his adolescent daughters.

He already knew that, but at ages twelve and fourteen they were still just kids, and rejected ones at that.

Oh, not rejected by him. He loved them enough for both parents, but it wasn't the same. Young girls needed their mother more than anyone else in the world, and his girls' mother, his ex-wife, had left all of them two years ago without even bothering to say goodbye.

He took a deep breath in an effort to shut off that line of thinking. It still hurt too much, and he knew that a kindred pain tore through Gloria and Amber when they were confronted with it.

"Dammit, Dad, do you realize this is the fourth housekeeper who's quit since Marsha left us?" he ranted. "Whatever happened to the kindly middle-aged employee who kept the home clean, took care of the kids and was part of the family?"

Buck laughed. "She went back to school, got a college degree and is now supervisin' an office full of people. Domestic help is hard to find these days, and even harder to keep. Especially if they don't get any cooperation from the man of the house. You can't expect anyone to keep the place clean and the kids in line if you won't let her discipline them, or better yet, discipline them yourself."

Jim's nerves tightened defensively at the implied criticism as he continued up the steps and headed for the front door. "Aw, come on, Buck, they're not all that bad. Just a little headstrong."

Buck was a small man, barely five foot eight inches compared to his son's six-two, and his face was craggy and lined from almost sixty years of farming in the high, thin mountain air of northern Idaho. He habitually dressed in faded jeans and shirts with well-worn boots and his ever-present Stetson hat, but underneath the "old cowhand" act he was sharp, energetic and feisty.

"It might seem that way to you and me," he admitted and followed his son into the house, shutting the door behind him. "We both love 'em and know they're hurtin' deep inside, but they have to learn to live in the world the way it is, not the way we wish it was, and that means bein' considerate of others."

"I know, but—"

Buck didn't wait for Jim to finish. "What you need, sonny, is another wife—"

"A wife!" Jim stopped abruptly on his way through the dining room to the kitchen and turned to face his father. His roar was a mixture of indignation and righteous wrath. "Like hell I do, and you of all people should understand that! After the way Marsha ran out on me and the kids I'll never trust another woman. Especially not with the well-being of my daughters."

Buck put up his hand in a sign of peace, but he neither blanched nor backed down under the intimidation of his towering son. Buck knew there was about as much menace in Jim as you'd find in a big friendly pussycat. He only turned into a tiger in self-defense or to protect someone else, and even then he could usually talk his way out of a confrontation instead of resorting to violence.

"You shouldn't blame all women for Marsha's mistakes, Jimmy. Why don't you measure them against your mother instead, God rest her soul? She was a saint." Even after all these years since his wife's death, talking about her still brought a quiver to Buck's voice.

In spite of Jim's chagrin a tender little smile lifted the corners of his mouth. "I guess she was as close to a saint as any of us mortals will ever get," he admitted softly, "but where am I going to find a wife like her in the Copper Canyon, Idaho, of today? The only women my age around here are married. The single ones are all teenagers or elderly widows. The kids graduating from high school either go off to college and never come back, or leave to go to the city and find jobs. There's really nothing to keep them in this isolated little farm town. In case you hadn't noticed, Dad, there's a critical shortage of marriageable women around here."

Buck took off his Stetson and scratched his head. "I may be gettin' old, but I'm not blind. Neither am I in the market for a wife, but you've got two daughters to raise, and they need a mother. Besides, you need a woman, too. You're too damn young to spend the rest of your life alone."

Jim sighed. "Young? I'm thirty-five going on fifty, and at times like this I feel eighty. Being married is no way to stay young. At least, not being married to Marsha."

He knew he sounded bitter, but that's because he was. He'd spent too many hours trying to comfort his heartbroken daughters in the years since their mother left. They couldn't understand why she just took off one day while they were in school and he was out in the fields without even telling them she was leaving.

Neither could he. Oh, they'd had their differences like any married couple, but they hadn't even quarreled the day she left. He came home to find a note telling him she'd cleaned out their bank account and was going to the city to "find herself." He'd tracked her down, but she'd refused to come back and had asked him to file for divorce. Since then the only communication she'd had with her daughters was cards on their birthdays and a gift apiece at Christmas, and it nearly tore him apart to see their pain and not be able to make it go away.

Buck's voice broke into his musing. "But that's what I'm tryin' to tell you. Not all women are like your ex-wife, and I've found a way for you to get one without ever leavin' home."

Jim turned and walked into the kitchen. "Enough, Buck. I don't even want to hear it. Let's change the subject. Did the girls get off to school all right?"

Again Buck followed behind him. "Yeah, but don't forget this is the day Gloria has basketball practice and Amber has a Camp Fire girl's meeting so they'll be late gettin' home this afternoon. Hey, if you got a few minutes I want to show you this magazine.''

Jim picked up the electric percolator and started making coffee. "What magazine...? No, on second thought, don't tell me. I don't want to know."

"It's right here, Jimmy," Buck said and waved a magazine that he'd seemingly produced from nowhere. "Someone brought it in to Red's Barber Shop a couple of weeks ago, and the guys have all been readin' through it and talkin' about it."

Red's Barber Shop was the gathering place for the older men of the community. Red Wannamaker had owned the establishment for more than forty years, and although the hair color that gave him his nickname had turned to gray, his shop was still a bastion of time-honored male bonding.

"Ain't no women allowed in my place" was his outspoken motto. Red had nothing but contempt for unisex hairstyling salons. "I'm a barber, and barbers only work on men," he informed anyone who challenged his discriminatory practice.

It was a moot point because Annabelle Hunt had owned Annie's Cut 'n' Curl Beauty Shoppe in the next block for almost as long, and her clients were equally senior in age. No man had ever set foot in her salon except to pick up his wife. Both she and her ladies would have been scandalized to have a male invade their privacy by insisting on having his hair cut there.

Jim plugged in the coffeepot. "Don't tell me you guys are circulating dirty magazines among yourselves," he said with amusement.

"Nah, this isn't dirty," Buck assured him. "It's put out by a service club that helps men and women who want to meet members of the opposite sex get together."

Jim's eyebrows arched and his jaw dropped as he turned to look at his father who had taken a seat at the kitchen table. "You mean a dating service? But you don't have to advertise for that. There are a lot of women your age right here who would go out with you in a minute if you'd just ask them.''

Buck waved the magazine at him. ''Not me!'' he said impatiently. ''You! I'm talkin' about brides. The men and women in here are lookin' for a marriage partner.''

Jim was beginning to feel like a weather vane in a storm. ''Are you saying you want me to order a bride out of a catalog?''

''No! Well...maybe it might seem that way, but this magazine has some really good-soundin' young women who want a husband, home and children. You said that's what you were looking for.''

''I said no such thing,'' Jim denied testily as he walked across the room and sat down at the table with Buck. ''I was talking about a housekeeper. You're the one who brought up the subject of marriage.'' He put out his hand. ''Let me see that magazine.''

In Eureka, California, Coralie Dixon sat slumped in her car parked across the street from the ruins of the apartment building that had been her home until the earthquake toppled it less than twenty-four hours before. She swallowed a sob and blinked back the tears that clouded her blue eyes. She'd done all the crying she intended to. All that got her was red eyes and a load of self-pity. It was time to get on with her life and that's exactly what she intended to do.

''I just don't understand,'' she said to her best friend, Kirsten Reinhold, who sat in the passenger seat next to her. ''I'm beginning to wonder if there's something in my genetic makeup that attracts earthquakes. This is the third time in my twenty-two years of life that I've been wiped out by a California temblor, and I'm getting awfully darn tired of it.''

"The *third* time?" Kirsten questioned. "I know you came up here to Eureka after the quake of '92 in Los Angeles, but when was the first time?"

Coralie leaned her head back against the seat and closed her eyes. "I was born in San Francisco and lived there until after Mom and Dad lost everything in the 1989 Loma Prieta earthquake. Shortly after that Dad's company transferred him to Los Angeles. We'd been there less than three years when the quake of '92 destroyed most of our possessions. That time my parents gave up and moved back to the Midwest where they'd been born and raised and still had lots of family. I came up here to Eureka."

She shivered. "I thought I'd be safe. I didn't know they had earthquakes up here."

Kirsten shook her head. "We usually don't. At least nothing more than a ripple, but unfortunately the whole state of California sits on a series of faults deep in the bowels of the earth. You're right, the upper northern part of the state is fairly immune, but apparently it can happen anywhere."

Coralie clenched the steering wheel with both hands. "Well, it's not going to happen to me again," she said angrily. "I'm getting out. Out of the town and out of the state. I'm going to go someplace where there's never been an earthquake before."

Kirsten chuckled wryly. "Well, good luck on finding such a haven, but until you do you're welcome to stay with me. I have an extra bedroom. Your building is unsafe and cordoned off so you can't go back there."

That made tears brim in Coralie's eyes again—tears of gratitude—and once more she blinked to keep them from spilling over. Kirsten was the dearest friend she'd ever had. They'd met two years before when Coralie, a nurse, first arrived in Eureka and went to work at the local hospital. Kirsten, also a nurse, worked there, too, and they'd hit it off right away.

She was a couple of years older than Coralie, and they sure didn't look anything alike. Coralie was fairly tall with long straight blond hair, blue eyes and a tendency to put on weight if she indulged in snacks or desserts, while Kirsten was shorter with a cap of dark curly hair, flashing brown eyes and the ability to eat all day without ever gaining a pound.

Their personalities were very similar, however, and their interests meshed nicely. They both liked country-and-western music, tearjerker movies and pizza, and now Kirsten was offering to give up her privacy in order to share her small two-bedroom house with Coralie.

"Darn it, you're going to make me cry again." She sniffed as her hand found Kirsten's and squeezed it. "That's awfully kind of you, but I don't want to crowd you. I know you like your privacy."

Kirsten grinned and squeezed Coralie's hand back. "Yeah, well, I'm not offering a lifetime residency. Just a place to bunk until you can find another digs of your own. Start the car and we'll go somewhere and have a key made for you."

As Coralie maneuvered through the streets still partially cluttered from the debris of fallen trees and building material, Kirsten broke the silence. "You didn't really mean what you said about moving out of California, did you?"

Coralie nodded vigorously. "I sure did. I'm tired of struggling to acquire nice things and then having it all come tumbling down around me. Three times is enough. I'm going to leave just as soon as I can gather my wits about me enough to make some plans."

"But where will you go?" Kirsten asked anxiously. "What will you do for money until you get resettled in another job? I don't mean to pry, but if your bank account is anything like mine it'll just about get you over the mountains and halfway across Nevada before it runs out.

She paused a moment, then added, "Or are you going to South Dakota where your parents are?"

Coralie shivered. "Lord, no! Not that Winner isn't a nice little town, but it's crawling with relatives who don't understand about independence and privacy. They'd all be telling me what to do with my life before I even got my things unpacked. They're nice, well-meaning people, including Dad and Mom, but I couldn't stand the interference."

She glanced at Kirsten. "You know what I mean?"

Her friend nodded. "Sure I do. Very few sons and daughters want to go back home to Mommy and Daddy once they've broken away, but still you can't just quit at the hospital and start out in the car with no job or destination in mind."

Coralie wished her friend wouldn't argue the matter. What she said made sense. Coralie knew it, but she didn't want to hear about it. She hadn't made any plans. All she knew was that she had to get away from this accursed state before it broke off from the rest of the continent and sank into the Pacific Ocean.

The following afternoon Kirsten came home from work with a magazine under her arm. "Here," she said as she tugged it free and handed it to Coralie. "I brought this home for you to look at. It's been circulating around the nurse's lounge for the past few days, and it occurred to me that it might be a solution to your problem."

Coralie looked at it. It was a semislick periodical called *Pairings*. The cover was a photo of a good-looking young couple gazing soulfully into each other's eyes. Probably a new confession-stories magazine, Coralie thought.

Totally bewildered, she asked her friend, "What problem do I have that this could solve?"

A sly grin split Kirsten's face. "It's a lonely-hearts club magazine, but a cut above the usual. Has some pretty good articles on how to meet and charm a member of the opposite sex, but mostly it's personal ads. You know," and she quoted theatrically, "Single male, handsome, steady job, loves to dance, looking for single professional woman, forty-inch bust, good cook. Object, matrimony."

Coralie blinked and looked at the magazine again, then back at Kirsten. "Kirsten Reinhold, what's gotten into you! Surely you're not suggesting that I answer one of those ads! I'm not in the market for a husband, and even if I were I sure wouldn't order one from a magazine."

Kirsten laughed. "Oh, I don't know," she said gleefully. "There's one in there says he looks like Paul Newman and has six beautiful kids who need a mother."

Coralie chuckled. "You nut. I didn't know you'd taken to reading fairy tales."

Kirsten assumed a serious demeanor, but her eyes sparkled. "Now you've hurt my feelings. Don't be so quick to reject the Paul Newman look-alike. I doubt that the real one is going to come knocking at your door, and it's about time you started thinking seriously about settling down."

Coralie rolled her eyes. "With Paul and his six kids? I think not. That guy's looking for a free nanny, housekeeper and bed partner, and you know I don't do windows."

She handed the publication back to Kirsten and started toward the kitchen. "Now come on, I fixed spaghetti for dinner and I don't want the garlic bread to get cold."

Kirsten brought the magazine to the table with her and halfway through the meal she mentioned the subject again. "You know, Coralie, I joked about the mail order bride idea, but I really do think you should give it some thought. That's why I brought the magazine to you. At least read it. The person who runs an ad has to fill out a long questionnaire about his or her likes, dislikes, temperament and family history. There's a copy of it in the back. It's all computerized so they can match you up with someone compatible."

Coralie wasn't having any of it. "Sure, provided the person filling out the questionnaire tells the truth. Do they do background checks?"

"I don't know," Kirsten admitted, "but you don't do a background check on every man you go out with, do you?"

"No, but you said these people are looking for marriage partners. I sure wouldn't marry a man I'd never met until the day before the wedding."

Kirsten sighed with exasperation. "That's not how it works. If you find a man in there who looks promising you write to the club and ask for his résumé. They'll send it along with his address and you can write to him. From then on it's up to the two of you whether or not you get together."

Coralie knew she wasn't going to pursue this matter, but her curiosity was piqued. She dabbed at her mouth with her napkin and held out her hand. "Okay, you win. Give it here and I'll take a look at it, but I can tell you now I'm not going to contact any of them."

Kirsten smiled as she passed the magazine over. "Of course not," she agreed. "Oh, by the way, I've circled a few that I thought might interest you."

The smug look on her friend's face made Coralie want to throw the periodical at her, but she contented herself with tossing it aside and changing the subject.

Later that night after Kirsten had gone to bed Coralie sat on the sofa and opened the magazine that had become such a big issue between the two women. The front and back covers were slick, but the inside pages were a good grade bond. It was printed in black-and-white.

She settled back and started turning the pages. The first part was devoted to articles that would probably be of interest to men and women looking for a mate, and a letters-to-the-editor section from couples who had met each other through the club, married and apparently were living happily ever after.

She skimmed over these and moved on to the ads, surprised at how many there were from both men and women, and how detailed they were. Some even included pictures. Were all these people really serious about marrying a stranger?

One picture in particular caught her eye. A blond Viking who looked as if he'd leapt off the cover of a historical romance. Why would a man who looked like him have to advertise for a wife? Probably some poor guy who didn't have much going for him in the looks department had sent in someone else's photo.

She noted the ads Kirsten had circled, but it wasn't until the last page that she found one that captured her interest. There was no picture, and only a brief description of himself and his accomplishments. Not enough to make an impression, but still it did. She couldn't explain why. It was just a feeling that she'd like to know more about this man.

Oh, well, why not? If she wrote to the club for his longer résumé, as they called it, it would please Kirsten, and she wouldn't have to contact him if she wasn't impressed.

Once more her gaze returned to the magazine in her lap and she picked it up and read:

Divorced male. Farmer in northern Idaho. Age 35. 6 ft. 2 in. Black hair, brown eyes. Two daughters, ages 12 and 14. Would like to hear from single woman, age 30 to 40. No children. Must like teenagers.

Chapter Two

Coralie's heart raced as she exited the plane that had brought her to Lewiston, Idaho, and walked into the airport terminal. She'd never flown before getting on the aircraft in San Francisco earlier that day. When she was growing up and she and her parents had visited the relatives in South Dakota, they'd always driven the car, so this was her maiden flight.

It was both exciting and unnerving. Exciting because it was all so new, and unnerving because she never should have let Kirsten talk her into accepting Jim Buckley's invitation to come for a "get-acquainted interview" in the first place. Kirsten had convinced her that she had nothing to lose since she'd already lost everything in the earthquake, and besides, it would be a great adventure.

Now she'd pretty well burned her bridges behind her. She'd somehow gotten caught up in this so-called adventure and had gone too far with it to go back. Besides, Mr. Buckley had invested too much time and money for her to hide out in the ladies' rest room until she could catch the next plane out.

No, since she'd been the one to make contact with him by answering his ad, she owed it to him to at least meet with him and tell the man in person that she'd changed her mind.

Quickly, she followed the signs to the luggage area where they'd agreed to meet. She had to admit she was curious. She wanted to know what a man who would advertise for a bride was really like. They'd exchanged pictures and a couple of letters apiece, but she knew better than most that didn't mean much. Pictures could lie, and so could letters.

Her picture was a lie, and she'd been less than truthful in her letters to him. Since she was so much younger than he'd specified in his ad, she'd sent him a picture of her Aunt Ellen, her mother's younger sister. She and Ellen looked a lot alike, but her aunt was fifteen years older than Coralie and about ten pounds heavier. She was still very pretty, and fit Coralie's description.

Then when she got the first letter from him and foolishly answered it she just conveniently "forgot" to tell him how old she was.

Coincidentally, his picture wasn't any better than hers. It probably was him all right, but it was taken at a distance and he was wearing a wide-brimmed Stetson hat that left his face too shadowed to tell what he looked like.

Jim raced into the airport parking lot and impatiently drove up and down the aisles until he finally found a place to park. He jumped out of the Cherokee, slamming the door behind him, and ran toward the terminal. Grabbing at his Stetson as a blast of frigid wind threatened to blow it off, he huddled deeper inside his heavy jacket. God it was cold. The clouds were getting darker and more threatening, and according to his watch Coralie Dixon's plane had touched down half an hour ago.

She probably thought he'd changed his mind about interviewing a total stranger for the position of wife and had left her stranded in an unfamiliar airport hundreds of miles from home. Well, it wasn't *his* mind that needed changing, it was his father's. It was bad enough that a usually sensible man like Buck would sign up his own son with a mail order marriage-partners club without telling him. But to have picked a woman in California from among the respondents and actually sent her a ticket to fly out for a meeting with his son made Jim seriously doubt Buck's sanity.

When his dad finally told him last night what he'd done it was too late for Jim to stop the woman. No one answered the phone at the number Buck had for her, so all they knew was that she planned to be on the flight from San Francisco this afternoon.

The last straw had been that multiple-car accident he'd encountered on the icy road just the other side of Cottonwood that held up traffic for more than an hour. Now he was late and Ms. Dixon must be sure that she'd been abandoned.

It was odd. Buck had shown him a picture she'd sent, and she was not only pretty, but she looked like a fairly sophisticated and well-educated woman, aged thirtysomething. He couldn't figure out why she would have to answer an ad for a mail order bride. On the other hand Buck said he'd sent a picture of Jim to her, and Jim hoped he wasn't so unappealing that he looked as if he couldn't get a wife on his own if he wanted one. Which he didn't!

Coralie sat on a bench in the luggage area with her suitcase at her feet and shifted nervously. She felt the stirring of panic, but was determined not to give in to it. So her knight in shining armor hadn't met the plane as he'd promised and was now forty-five minutes late. He had to drive to Lewiston from his farm near a place called Copper Canyon, so maybe he got lost, or had a flat tire, or...

Or maybe he was a weirdo who got his jollies out of enticing naive young women into taking long trips to see him and then standing them up. But she was neither naive nor stupid, she'd just let herself get caught up in the spirit of adventure that Kirsten so glowingly painted. Still, she'd decided to take the next flight out, anyway, so if he didn't show it would save her the embarrassment of telling him she'd changed her mind.

Apparently, he'd changed his, too. Well, she'd give him another fifteen minutes, then she'd go to the desk and arrange to get another ticket. After all, Mr. James Buckley was paying for her little jaunt, and if that's the way he wanted to spend his money who was she to complain? She'd gotten her first airplane trip for free.

The sound of running feet interrupted her thoughts, and she looked up to see a man hurrying into the area. There was luggage from another plane coming up now, and he stopped and looked around the crowd retrieving their bags. Her heart speeded up, and she had a totally unsubstantiated intuition that this was the man she was waiting for.

At least, she hoped it was. If so, she sure wasn't going to be on the next flight out. She wanted to get to know this guy better. He looked like every woman's dream prince. Tall, and even though he wore a sheepskin-lined denim jacket she could see that his jeans-encased hips and legs were slender and muscular.

Her excitement escalated. This could well be Jim Buckley. He fit the description. He was carrying his Stetson so she could see his black hair cut short at the sides but a little longer on top. He hadn't told her in his letters how ruggedly handsome he was with those big, dark brown eyes that roamed back and forth over the crowd but never seemed to make contact with her.

Maybe she hadn't been too foolhardy, after all.

Jim stood at the edge of the group of recently discharged passengers who were waiting for their luggage. He knew none of these would be from Ms. Dixon's flight, he was too late for that, but surely she was still waiting for him somewhere around here. Where else could she go? If they didn't meet here where Buck had arranged for them to, how would they ever find each other?

His gaze scanned the outer edges of the room. There were people coming and going, but none that looked enough like her picture or description to be her. There was an attractive blond teenager sitting on a bench against the wall, looking lost and obviously waiting for somebody, but that couldn't be Coralie Dixon. This one was much too young.

He walked slowly through the crowd, trying to get a closer look at the women milling around, and at the same time hoping Ms. Dixon would see and recognize him. He hadn't seen the picture of himself that Buck had sent her, but his dad said it was one he'd snapped with the Polaroid camera when Jim wasn't aware of it. Knowing Buck's questionable talent with a camera he probably cut off Jim's head, or got the whole picture out of focus.

Halfway through his second promenade someone tapped his shoulder, and a woman's voice said, "Excuse me. Are you by any chance James Buckley from Copper Canyon, Idaho?"

He turned and looked down into the wide, blue eyes of the kid who had been sitting on the bench. He blinked. "Yes, I'm Jim. Is there something I can do for you?"

She looked relieved. "I'm Coralie. Coralie Dixon from Eureka, California. I was beginning to think you weren't coming."

Jim did a mental double take. Just what was this girl trying to pull? "Look, young lady. You're about twenty years too young to be the woman who presented herself to me as Coralie Dixon, so suppose you tell me what's going on."

She cringed, but didn't back down. "I'm sorry. I misled you about my age, but I am Coralie. I have identification if you'll just give me a minute to find it."

She was carrying a suitcase, which she set down on the floor, then shrugged the long strap of her purse off her shoulder. Up close he could see her smooth, creamy skin and the soft full lips that looked eminently kissable. She was wearing navy blue slacks with a tailored jacket to match. A silk blouse underneath was colorful in shades of blue and red, and over her arm she carried a lightweight all-weather coat.

Flabbergasted by her confession Jim picked up the case and took her by the arm. My God, this whole experience was like a comedy of errors, but there was nothing funny about it.

He led her back to the bench and sat her down, then put the suitcase on the floor at their feet and sat down beside her. She rummaged in her purse and came up with a card, which she handed to him. It was a driver's license with a picture of a pretty young woman with wide blue eyes and long straight blond hair that was parted in the middle and cascaded down her back.

It was her all right. The information revealed that she was Coralie Elizabeth Dixon, age twenty-two, weight of 130 pounds and the address in Eureka, California, that matched the one Buck had for the woman he'd been corresponding with using Jim's name.

Dear God, his dad may have had the best of intentions, but he'd really screwed up this time. Not only had he been totally off base in registering Jim in that lonely-hearts club without Jim's knowledge, but he'd been responsible for transporting this...this *child* across state lines with a promise of marriage.

Jim didn't care what her driver's license said, she didn't look a day older than eighteen, and she wouldn't be the first teenager to lie about her age. It would have been awkward enough if Buck had wanted her for himself, but to have lured her here to trap his son into a marriage with her.... Damn! Both he and Buck could be in real trouble if this girl turned out to be *under* eighteen!

Jim was jolted out of his angry thoughts when she spoke again. "Mr. Buckley...uh, Jim, I'm sorry I wasn't exactly truthful about my age, but I didn't think it would be all that important."

She sounded apologetic, and well she should be. He didn't take kindly to being lied to, but unfortunately she'd been misinformed also. He shouldn't take his frustration out on her. It was Buck he was going to have words with when he got home.

He looked into those upturned blue eyes and sighed. She really was a beauty. He couldn't help but wonder why she'd answered an ad for a mail order bride. Surely she had men waiting in line to marry her, if that's what she wanted, or at least to take her out and show her a good time. Especially if she really was twenty-two.

"It is important, Coralie," he said, using her first name in an effort to sound less judgmental, "but that's not the only problem. Someone else using my name put that ad in the magazine. I'm not looking for a wife—"

Her mouth fell open. "But you wrote to me—"

"No, I'm sorry, I didn't. You received letters from the person using my name. I didn't know anything about it until last night when he told me what he'd done and that you were arriving today, expecting to marry me."

That seemed to snap her out of her shock, and he watched her expression change from guilt to annoyance. "I did not come here expecting to marry you. I was just going to be here a short time so we could get acquainted in person. There were no plans for a quick wedding."

He liked the crisp snap in her voice and the fire in her eyes. Maybe she was older than he'd thought, after all. "Yes, of course, that's what I meant. I'm as shocked as you because I only learned about this whole scheme to get me married after it was too late to stop you from coming."

"Is that why you were so slow getting here?" She sounded angry, and he knew she thought he'd deliberately kept her waiting.

"No, believe me, I left Copper Canyon in plenty of time to meet your plane, but there was an accident on the highway that tied up traffic for nearly an hour. I got here just as quick as I could once that was cleared up."

Coralie didn't know whether to berate or reassure him. Was he telling her the truth? Or was it all a giant deception? A joke to laugh about once the poor woman who was so hard up for a husband that she'd come all the way from California to marry a stranger had been turned away.

She felt like a fool, and the heat of humiliation burned all through her. Apparently, she wasn't as grown up as she'd thought. It didn't take him long to catch on to her little deception. He'd accused her of being too young before he even asked her age.

"Who was this person who placed that ad in the magazine without your knowledge or permission?" she demanded. "He or she should be reported to the proper authorities."

Jim hesitated. Although he intended to sear the hide off Buck with a tongue lashing in private, he wasn't going to expose his father to public ridicule and possibly even criminal charges. Buck hadn't meant any harm. He'd only been trying to fix his son up with a suitable wife and got carried away.

"It doesn't matter who it was," he said. "I'll take care of it and see to it that it doesn't happen again. You will, of course, be reimbursed for any expense you've been put to. You do have a return ticket, don't you?"

Coralie opened her purse. "I have a cashier's check for the amount. You, I mean, whoever it was that contacted me, sent it."

Jim shook his head and regretted the bitterness in her tone. "Well, I'm glad the person responsible for this was thoughtful enough to send you fare for both ways. If you'll come with me I'll arrange to get you out of here on the next flight to San Francisco."

She got the check out of her purse and handed it to him, then trailed along beside him as he strode toward the reservation counter. She almost had to run to keep up. His long legs measured nearly one stride to her two, and she wasn't exactly short. The top of her head came about to his shoulder, but she was wearing flat-heeled pumps with her slacks while his boots had heels that put him well over six feet.

At the counter he gave the clerk the check and explained that Ms. Dixon would like to book a seat on the next flight to San Francisco.

"No, Jim, wait—" Coralie interrupted, but the clerk shook her head.

"All flights out of here have just been grounded indefinitely," she told them. "We've had a winter storm warning for the past hour. There's a blizzard bearing down on us, and we won't be able to take off or land planes until it blows itself out. We've been told to advise passengers that there could be long delays."

Jim frowned. Damn. He was going to have to put her up at a hotel overnight. It wasn't the expense he objected to, but he felt responsible for her. He still wasn't convinced she was old enough to find her own way back to California. If he just left her alone in a hotel and something happened to her he'd never forgive himself.

He glanced at her standing beside him. She looked more than a little shaken. "Have you done much traveling?"

She shook her head. "Not much. This is my first airplane trip." She looked around her. "Will I have to stay here in the airport all that time until the plane leaves?"

He bit back an expletive. The poor kid was an inexperienced traveler and unsure of how to proceed. It wasn't her fault, and he wished now he'd insisted that Buck meet her and send her back. He's the one who should be handling this problem. Maybe then he wouldn't be so quick to meddle again.

Jim forced himself to smile. "No, of course not," he said. "There's a hotel near the airport. I'll get you a room and give you enough money to tide you over while you wait there. Will you be all right?"

"Well, I . . ." Her voice was unsteady, but she straightened her shoulders, dampened her lips with her tongue and cleared her throat. "Yes, of course I'll be all right. I told you, I'm not a child. I'll be just fine."

Jim could tell that she wasn't as sure of that as she wanted him to think she was, and he couldn't blame her. It could be downright dangerous for a beautiful young woman waiting alone for hours in an unfamiliar airport far away from home.

He felt the icy breath of alarm at the back of his neck. As a lifelong resident of Idaho, and a farmer at that, he knew better than to ignore blizzard warnings. This one might last for days and would not only keep planes from flying, but also close the country roads.

He had to get home! He'd left Buck with Gloria and Amber, but they might be snowed in for God knows how long. His dad couldn't handle everything that had to be done on a farm in a blizzard by himself, but neither could Jim leave this girl stranded all alone in the middle of a winter storm.

There was no time to look for options. He had to leave immediately in order to get back to Copper Canyon before heavy winds and snow made driving unsafe, if not impossible.

He turned to look at Coralie who had turned several shades paler. "I have to get back home before the storm hits, but I'm not going to leave you here alone for what could be several days. You'll have to come with me. We have no other choice.''

She gasped with surprise, but he continued on. "You needn't worry, we'll be well chaperoned. My dad and two daughters will be snowed in with us if it comes to that, and we've plenty of food and fuel. We natives prepare for the Idaho winters.''

Again he picked up her suitcase. "You'll want to put on your coat, and a hat and gloves if you have them. It's freezing outside.''

Coralie struggled to pull her thoughts together and make her own decisions about what she was going to do. "Now hold on there,'' she cried as he took her arm and tried to propel her along beside him. "I'm not going anywhere with you until I get answers to some very important questions. Such as, who wrote those letters to me if you didn't?''

He stopped and glared at her. "We can talk on the way. Right now it's imperative that we get started so we can get home before this storm gathers its full force.''

"No way!'' she said as she planted her feet firmly on the floor and shook his hand off her arm. "We'll talk right now. How do I know you're who you say you are? For that matter, I don't even have any proof that you have a father and two daughters, or a farm.''

Just talking about the possibilities for deception sent fingers of fear up her spine.

He glared at her, but then his expression softened and so did his tone of voice. "Okay, you've made your point. Let's go over there out of the way and sit down.''

He led her to a row of chairs. She sat down and he put her suitcase on the floor, then took his wallet from his back pocket and extracted several cards from it. "Here's my driver's license,'' he said and handed it to her. "Also my Visa card, a gas company credit card and my membership card in the local grange.''

He handed them each to her one at a time, then sat down and started rummaging in his other pockets. She looked closely at the driver's license. He was James Buckley, all right. The picture looked just like him, and the identification matched everything he'd told her. The other cards were in order, too, and she was about to give them back when he handed her two more. They were pictures.

"The top one is my two daughters. The oldest is Gloria and the younger one is Amber. Underneath is a picture of them with my dad. They were a little younger then, but you can tell it's the same kids."

The picture of the girls was a studio portrait of two strikingly attractive girls. The elder was dark and bore a strong family resemblance to Jim, but the younger one was small in stature with blond hair and blue eyes.

The second picture was an informal snapshot of the same two children with an older man. He didn't look like Jim, but he had an arm around each of the girls, and they were all laughing and happy. There was no reason to think he wasn't their grandfather.

She gave them all back to him. "You have beautiful daughters," she said, "and your identification checks out—"

"Then let's get going," he interrupted impatiently and started to get up.

"Not yet," she said, her tone as determined as his was impatient. "Not until you tell me who wrote those letters to me and sent the tickets. I get the feeling that you're trying to protect the culprit, and I want to know why."

Jim sighed and sat back down.

Taking a deep breath she continued her interrogation. "I need to know what's going on," she said. "If you didn't put that ad in the magazine and then write to me, who did? And why? I know it was dumb of me to answer it, but I did it in good faith. Isn't it against the law to place false advertisements in newspapers and magazines?"

He looked straight ahead, but she could tell that he was wrestling with her questions. When he eventually spoke, his tone was strained. "I suspect there is a law against that type of thing, yes, but please believe me that there was nothing criminal intended."

By now Coralie had recovered enough from the shock of this unreal experience to demand answers. "I'm sorry, but I don't believe you. Why else would anyone do such a thing? You apparently know why, and I'd just be getting myself in deeper by going home with you. Either tell me all you know about it or I'm staying right here no matter how long the delay."

Jim could tell that she believed she was in more danger with him than she would be waiting alone in Lewiston, and she had every right to. Not that he'd ever hurt her, but there were men out there who would. She'd already been put through enough embarrassment and inconvenience without him adding to her fear.

After all, it wasn't in any way her fault. Much as he wanted to protect Buck from the consequences of his misguided intrusion into his son's personal affairs, Jim couldn't let the girl suffer.

"You're right," he said. "You are entitled to the full story, but I hope you'll keep an open mind until you've heard it all. You see, it was my dad who put that ad in the magazine under my name."

Her exquisite blue eyes widened. "Your father! But why would he do a thing like that?"

Jim sighed. "Oh, as I told you he had the best of intentions. He thinks I should get married again."

"But what business is that of his?"

Jim shook his head. "Well, none, actually, but I do have two young daughters who need supervision, and we're having a hard time finding and keeping housekeepers."

She looked shocked. "So you brought me here under false pretenses," she accused angrily. "You were going to marry me only to get a housekeeper and a nanny for your children.''

Jim's hands clenched and he blew out his breath in exasperation. "Now just a darn minute," he grated. "I wasn't going to marry you, period. I told you, it was Dad who arranged this whole debacle without telling me anything about it.

"He's a crusty old romantic, although he'd never admit it. You might be flattered to know that he picked you out of the several dozen letters he received. He said you were the prettiest, the sweetest and the best qualified to help raise his precious granddaughters."

Coralie was appalled to discover that she was flattered, and she quickly pushed that feeling aside. "And how would he know how 'sweet' I am? He's never met or talked to me."

"I asked him that same question," Jim said. "He told me he could tell from the tone of your letters, and while we're on the subject, who are you to complain? At least he was being honest. Who's picture did you send him? It sure wasn't you."

She looked taken aback, and for a moment she hesitated. "No, you're right, it wasn't," she admitted sheepishly. "It was my Aunt Ellen, my mother's younger sister, but we look a lot alike."

"Your aunt!" he howled. "Why did you send her picture? She's a mighty pretty woman, but so are you."

"Be-because," Coralie stammered. "Your ad said you wanted a woman in her thirties, and if I'd sent a photo of me, you…you'd have known I was a lot younger than that."

He saw the blush of embarrassment that colored her cheeks, and she wouldn't meet his gaze. "In other words," he said, "you were being deliberately misleading. I think that's called using the mail to defraud, and that's also against the law so let's not have any more accusations. Dad was wrong to do what he did, but so were you. Did you lie about anything else?"

She had the grace to look ashamed. "No, and I didn't mean to 'defraud' anybody. Besides, what's wrong with a wife who's younger than you?"

She looked so much like a repentant child that he couldn't stay annoyed at her. "Nothing if that's what a man wants, but I've got two teenage daughters to raise, I don't need a child bride, too."

This time her head snapped up and she looked right at him. "I'm not a teenager, and you're way too young to be my father. Your ad said you're thirty-five, and your driver's license confirms it."

He nodded. "I am, and if you really are twenty-two that still makes you thirteen years younger than me. If I ever do decide to marry again it won't be to someone I have to raise."

"That's ageist," she snapped, obviously annoyed. "You're discriminating against me because of my age."

He chuckled. "Damn right I am, but it's not discrimination, it's just good common sense. I'm a farmer. That's a twenty-four-hour-a-day job and it'll never make me rich. I need a wife who is mature enough to understand and help me."

She sniffed. "If it's such long hours and poor pay why don't you quit and get a real job?"

Jim bit back an oath. She may not realize it, but every word she spoke just reinforced his insistence that she was too young and immature to appeal to him.

"You call me an ageist," he said, "but do you know what you are? You're an elitist."

She gasped. "I am not!"

"Oh, yes, you are. You come out here to this rugged country wearing designer clothes and two-inch-long red fingernails and impatiently tell me, a farmer who raises wheat so you can have bread, to get a *real job*. What in hell is that if not elitist?"

She looked startled. "I ... I didn't mean it that way, and my clothes were bought off the rack from a department store. I work hard, too."

He glanced at her lap where her small white hands were nervously entwined. "With those fingernails?"

Again she blushed and looked away from him. "They...they're false. I just had them put on yesterday. My own are quite short."

Now he felt like a bully. How did she manage to stir so many different emotions in him in such a short time? He reached over and squeezed both of her hands in one of his. Hers were soft and warm, and his stomach muscles tightened at their touch. "Hey, I'm sorry. I was out of line. Don't apologize, you have beautiful hands."

She looked up then, and her mouth quivered. "No, I'm the one who was out of line. I didn't mean to insult you. What I meant to say was why don't you change jobs if farming is so hard."

He squeezed her hands again, then reluctantly released them. "Farming is hard, I can't deny that, but it's what I do. I was born to it. My people have farmed the land for generations, and I wouldn't be happy doing anything else."

His anxiety about the weather had been escalating, and again he shifted to stand. "Now if you're satisfied that I'm telling you the truth we really do have to be on our way. It's imperative that I get home this evening, even if it means driving in the worst of the storm, and I don't want to do that if I have you with me. If you still have doubts I'll take you to the hotel, but either way we have to get moving ... now."

Chapter Three

Coralie and Jim walked together in silence through the terminal and across the parking lot. Coralie shivered and clutched at Jim's arm as the cold wind blew right through her lightweight coat and whipped her shoulder-blade-length hair across her face. Unfortunately, she hadn't taken into account the fact that winters in Idaho lasted longer and were much colder than the ones in California. She was definitely not prepared for an Idaho blizzard.

Not only was her coat not heavy enough, but she'd packed her knit hat and gloves in her suitcase along with her boots. She should have known better, but in California flowers were blooming and the temperatures were in the high sixties. She hadn't counted on wading through a couple of feet of snow once she arrived. And with more on the way yet!

Jim stopped at a big, dark brown-and-bronze all-terrain Jeep Cherokee. "Here we are," he said as he unlocked the door on the passenger side and helped her to climb in. It was high off the ground and he had to put both hands at her waist and boost her up. His hands were big and strong but gentle, and he lifted her 130 pounds without even a grunt. He'd written in his letters, or at least somebody had, that he raised wheat so he was probably used to hefting sacks of grain. There was no doubt about his muscle capacity.

He tossed her suitcase in the back, then walked around the vehicle and slid under the steering wheel. "It'll be warm in here in a minute," he said as he turned on the engine and the heater, then looked at her. "You must be freezing." His voice was brisk with concern. "Your face and hands are red with cold, and you're shivering. Here." He stripped off his leather fur-lined gloves and handed them to her. "Put these on. They'll help you to warm up faster."

"Oh, but you'll need them—"

"I'm used to the cold," he insisted and reached out to take her bare hands in his. His skin was rough but warm, and his heat radiated through her.

"Oh, that feels good," she said as his hands engulfed both of hers, and she realized it wasn't just his warmth she was talking about. His touch was strong and reassuring, as was the concern that looked out of his expressive brown eyes.

He seemed to really care about her predicament, unlike a lot of men who would think she deserved whatever she got if she was stupid or desperate enough to answer an ad for a mail order bride. Maybe her decision to go home with him had been the right one. She felt that she could trust this man, Jim Buckley, to keep her from harm until she could get away from here.

In a short time the chill was gone and the cab was warm and toasty. Jim insisted she put on his gloves, then backed the vehicle out of the parking space and headed away from the airport. Coralie leaned back and relaxed until they left the outskirts of Lewiston on their journey to Jim's farm and...

A new wave of apprehension swept over her, dispelling her short period of serenity, and she sat back up. And what? How far was it to Copper Canyon? She'd forgotten to ask him that. What would happen once they got there? How did she know he could be trusted to bring her back to the airport in Lewiston when the planes started flying again?

Maybe it wouldn't storm, after all, and she could leave tomorrow as planned. But what if it did and she couldn't? He'd said that a blizzard sometimes lasted for days in this section of the country. How much snow would it bring? How long would she be trapped with this man and his family?

Her thoughts were unsettling. There were so many things she should have asked about before she got in the car with this stranger. Instead, she'd let his clean-cut good looks and rugged charm entice her into going home with him when she didn't even know where "home" was. Idaho was a big state.

She cleared her throat. "Jim, how far is it to your farm from here?"

He smiled at her. "About eighty-five miles, but the last fourteen of it is on narrow unpaved roads that are nearly impassible in a blizzard. That's why I have to get there as quickly as possible."

That far She hadn't taken into account that airports were few and far between in Idaho.

It had started to snow and the wind had picked up, too. The low-hanging clouds were dark and threatening. Coralie shifted uneasily in the seat beside him. "Did you say your father lives with you?" she asked anxiously.

"Buck lives on the farm, but he has his own little house," Jim explained. "During a blizzard, though, he stays with the girls and me."

"How come you call your dad Buck?"

Jim shrugged. "I don't know. That's what everyone calls him. His name is Amos Buckley, but he's always been known as Buck. I picked up on it when I was a kid and he never objected. We're very close. He's one of my best friends as well as my dad, but don't get me wrong. That doesn't give him the right to meddle in my life the way he's done this time."

She chuckled. "He sounds like Kirsten."

"Who's Kirsten?"

"She's my best friend, and she's also the one who talked me into answering your ad. It looks like we were both manipulated by others into this oddball situation. Dare we call it fate?"

Jim was more inclined to call it interference, but he had the good sense not to say so.

Coralie relaxed back against the seat again and watched the scenery. She might as well see everything she could while she had the chance. It was doubtful that she'd ever come to Idaho again.

Snow covered the ground and the evergreen trees as they climbed rapidly out of the valley and up the winding highway into the gently rolling hills. As her plane had circled to land, the pilot had pointed out that the small city of Lewiston was the confluence of two rivers, the Clearwater and the Snake, and that it was an inland seaport with more than 450 miles of deep-water channel to the Pacific Ocean. It had been a pretty sight, including the huge round steel storage tanks that dotted the hillsides. The pilot said they held grain.

"Do you raise anything other than wheat on your farm?" she asked.

Jim looked at her and smiled. "We raise winter wheat, barley and lentils on a three-year rotation. This year it's wheat. We also have a garden and grow our own vegetables."

She shook her head in self-deprecation. "I hate to show how dumb I am, but I've been a city girl all my life. I really don't know anything about farming. Why do you plant different crops each year?"

"Don't ever be afraid to ask questions," Jim said. "That's the way you learn. We rotate our crops to renew the soil, otherwise it wears out. If you plant the same crop every year it drains the ground of certain minerals that a different crop will replace."

He chuckled at her puzzled expression. "It's a little hard to explain, but, trust me, it's a highly recommended conservation measure."

She laughed, too. He really was a nice man. He'd said just the right thing to put her at ease about being so uninformed.

There were other questions she wanted to ask, but before she could he sobered and cleared his throat. "Coralie, there's something you need to know." He sounded apprehensive, and all her doubts and fears returned. Now what?

"My girls don't know anything about you," he continued. "They won't know who you are or why I've brought you home with me. I didn't even know about you myself until yesterday, and when Buck told me you were coming I made it abundantly clear that I'd have nothing to do with his little scheme."

She flinched at the starkness of his words, and he must have noticed because his tone turned to regret. "No, please, don't take that personally. It had nothing to do with you. It was the idea I objected to. It's true there are few marriageable women in Copper Canyon, but I don't think my dad realizes how dangerous it can be to send for a man or woman you've never even met to be a marriage partner. He's lived all his life in rural Idaho where everybody is either close friends or related, and nobody has reason to lock their doors or assume someone is out to harm them."

Again Coralie cringed. She knew he didn't mean to criticize her, but even so every word was like a blow to her self-esteem.

She couldn't blame him. Everything he said was true. She was the one who had been foolish. She should never have answered that advertisement. If she hadn't been so upset about losing everything in an earthquake for the third time she wouldn't have, but she'd been so spooked, and in such a hurry to get out of California before one of the darn things finally killed her, that she panicked and used any excuse to flee.

She jumped when Jim's hand covered both of hers again, and his voice was filled with contrition when he spoke. "Honey, I'm sorry. I don't know what's the matter with me. No matter what I say it turns out wrong."

He squeezed her hands. "Believe me, I'm not scolding you for coming here. You had no way of knowing those letters weren't written by me. Fortunately, Buck's intentions were honorable even though his reasoning was way off base, and I'm certainly not going to harm you."

He peered at her with concern. "What I'm trying to do is explain why my kids are going to be surprised when I bring you home with me. Since I made it very plain to Buck that I was going to put you on the next flight back to San Francisco we saw no reason to mention this little episode to the girls. They're going to wonder who you are, and why you're with me. I need to get it straight about what you want me to tell them."

Her eyes widened. "What *I* want you to tell them?"

"Well, yeah," he said. "Unless you want me to tell them the truth we'll have to make up a story. I just thought you might prefer to do it since you're the only one who knows what excuse you'd be most comfortable with."

Coralie sighed. She'd agreed to come here partly because she wanted adventure, and she was getting it in spades! She'd had nothing but shocks and surprises ever since she'd stepped off that plane. Now she had to think up a plausible lie to tell Jim's impressionable daughters since the fact that she'd come here as a possible mail order bride for their father wasn't likely to sit all that well with them.

She was beginning to think she'd have been better off to take her chances with the earthquakes in California.

"When you left this morning what did you tell them you were going to Lewiston for?" she asked.

"I didn't tell them I was going to Lewiston. They went to school before I left, and I expected to be back before they got home."

He hesitated, and when he spoke again he sounded agitated. "I don't know what Buck's told them, but I'm sure he wouldn't tell them I'd gone to Lewiston. Now I'm going to have to outright lie to them."

Coralie was warmed by a strong feeling that he didn't often hide things from his children or deliberately mislead them. "Are you uncomfortable with that?" she asked.

"Damn right I am," he answered gruffly. "I don't let them get away with lying to me or telling me half-truths, but I don't do that to them, either."

He shifted restlessly in his seat. "Unfortunately, in this case the truth is apt to do more harm that a well-thought-out lie. Their grandfather and I wouldn't be very good role models if they found out what has really been going on."

Again she twisted her hands together. "And I sure wouldn't come across as a good role model if they found out I'd answered an ad for a mail order bride to a man I'd never met."

He glanced at her, then looked away. "I'm afraid we're all three going to look like fools if this ever gets out."

Coralie thought so, too. "Then we'll have to see that it never does," she said briskly. "How about if we tell them you've just hired me as your new housekeeper? You said you were having trouble finding and keeping them."

Jim thought about that for a moment, then shook his head. "No, that wouldn't work. You'll only be with us a few days at the most and then you'll leave. How would we explain that? Our past housekeepers haven't stayed long, but each of them lasted several months before quitting."

She wanted to ask why they all quit, but decided it was none of her business. Instead, she cast around in her mind again for a more plausible story. They drove along in silence for several miles before an idea struck her.

"I know," she said and perked up immediately. "Why don't we tell them what really happened to us at the airport? That we met there and found out that I was going to be stuck for possibly days so you brought me home with you to wait out the storm. We'd only have to make a few 'adjustments' to the truth."

Jim frowned. "Yes, but what would I have been doing at the airport, and what excuse could I have for bringing a woman I'd met casually only minutes before home with me? There'll be a lot of strangers waiting it out in the airport if this blizzard is as bad as it's reported to be."

Coralie was getting into the swing of plotting this story, and she was sure it had possibilities. "Don't be so quick to dismiss it," she said. "We can work out the knots. You could tell the girls you had to drive into Lewiston to pick up a package at the airport. Something you'd ordered through the mail."

Jim shook his head. "If I'd ordered anything it would come through the post office or United Parcel. I wouldn't have to pick it up at the airport."

She was only stopped for a moment until another thought bounced into her mind. "Do your daughters know that?"

He paused. "Well, no, I don't suppose they do, but—"

"Then what difference does it make? They won't question it. And as for my being a stranger, why can't I be somebody you knew in the past. Did you go to college?"

He nodded. "I have a degree in agriculture from the university in Moscow, but what's that got to do with—"

"You can tell them I'm a woman you knew in college and we just happened to run into each other...."

Her words trailed off as she realized he was laughing.

She turned to him. "What's so funny?" she demanded.

He returned her gaze, but his was filled with both amusement and tenderness. "You are," he said softly. "Honey, don't you realize that when I was a senior in college you were all of nine years old?"

Oh, damn, the age difference again. She had to admit it did sound pretty daunting when put like that. It ruled out the possibility of passing her off as an old college chum for sure, but that had been thirteen years ago. Now they were both adults and age shouldn't matter anymore as far as their relationship was concerned. At least, it didn't to her.

On second thought that wasn't altogether true. It did matter to her, but only because he refused to see her as anything but a child not much older than his elder daughter.

"Coralie, I'm sorry," he said and roused her from her musing. "I shouldn't have laughed. Did I hurt your feelings? I didn't mean to. It's just that I had this picture in my mind of me towering over you at six feet two, leading all four feet or so of you with long braids, skinned knees and a teddy bear in one arm around the campus by the hand. We'll have to find some other way to have met in your story."

She smiled at his description, but didn't really think it was funny. "That's all right," she assured him. "You didn't hurt my feelings. It's just that..." She paused, trying to find the right words and wondering if she shouldn't just drop it before she said more than she intended to.

"Just what?" he asked, looking concerned.

She took a deep breath. "Just that you let this age thing keep you from taking me seriously."

His brow furrowed. "I'm sorry you think that. Actually, I take you very seriously. That's why I'm bringing you home with me instead of leaving you to ride out the storm in a hotel room all by yourself. I want you where I can take care of you."

Take care of you. Coralie could have screamed with frustration. Not that she had anything against being taken care of by the right man, one who would love her and whom she could love and take care of in return. But Jim felt obligated to look after her like he looked after his children. He didn't see her as a woman, but as a young girl whom he was responsible for.

They continued to refine the story they'd tell Jim's daughters as they drove along the paved highway. The Cherokee was warm inside, and it was heavy enough to withstand the raging wind without too much swaying. Coralie was caught up in their conversation and sort of lost track of the storm until they came to a small town called Grangeville and stopped at a gas station. It was only then that she realized it was getting dark.

"Sorry we can't stop long enough to have something to eat," he said, "but the wind is getting stronger and the snow thicker. It won't be long before our visibility is zero, and I don't want to take the chance of getting caught in the middle of nowhere and unable to see. There are rest rooms and vending machines inside if you want to take advantage of them."

Jim got out of the Cherokee and walked around it to help Coralie. Damn, the wind was even stronger than he'd thought, and colder, too. She had the door open on her side and he held out his arms to help her, then kept one arm around her waist and held her against his side as they fought the wind on the quick run to the station.

There was something awfully nice about that brief physical contact, and once inside he hated to release her. He did, however, and greeted the two attendants who were acquaintances of his, as were most of the residents of Grangeville, then went over to the public telephone and dialed his home number. He knew Buck and the girls would be worried about him being so late, and he wanted to put their minds at ease.

A familiar female voice answered on the second ring. "Hi, Gloria, this is Dad—"

"Dad, are you okay?" She sounded both fearful and relieved. "We expected you back hours ago. We were afraid you'd gotten caught in the storm somewhere—"

"I'm fine, honey," he hastened to assure her. "I had to go into Lewiston and was held up longer than I'd expected."

"Lewiston? What were you doing there?"

"I'll tell you all about it when I get home, but right now let me talk to Grandpa."

"Grandpa's out in the barn feeding the animals," she explained. "When will you be home?"

Oh, hell. He'd wanted to warn Buck that he was bringing Coralie with him and clue his dad in on the story they were going to tell the girls. "I'm in Grangeville, and I'll be leaving for home as soon as I hang up. Tell Grandpa that when he comes in, and tell him also that we'll, um, that is, *I'll* be slow getting home because of the force of the storm. And, Gloria, tell him to stay inside. I'll do anything else that has to be done around the farm when I get there."

Coralie didn't see Jim at first when she came out of the rest room, but then she caught a glimpse of him out of the window, pumping gas into the Cherokee. There was an overhanging roof over the front of the station and the pumps, which afforded a small measure of protection from the elements to anyone under it. She felt a twinge of guilt when she realized that she was wearing his warm gloves and he was holding that icy metal nozzle in his bare hands.

She pulled the gloves off and started toward the door to give them to him when it opened and he came stomping in. He caught sight of her and rubbed his cold hands together as he smiled. "Are you ready to leave?"

She held the gloves out to him. "Yes, but I'm not going to budge until you put these on. You should have asked me for them before you went out to pump that gas."

His smile widened to a grin. "Yes, Mama," he said and took them from her as he bent his head and kissed her on the cheek.

His face was cold, but his lips were warm and sent a corresponding heat surging through her. She could feel the blush that colored her face, but before she could react he bent down and scooped her up in his arms. "Put your arms around my neck and hang on," he ordered. "Your feet are getting wet, and I'm not going to take a chance of the wind blowing you away from me."

She did as he instructed and buried her face in his sheepskin collar as he strode out the door, made his way to the Cherokee and tucked her neatly inside. She huddled on the seat and shivered as he got in on the other side.

"Are you all right?" he asked anxiously.

"Don't worry about me," she said through chattering teeth. "Just get me to wherever we're going as soon as possible. I've never been in a blizzard before. I had no idea it would be anything like this. I'm sorry now that I held you up back at the airport, even for a little while."

He started the engine and headed out of town on a narrow bumpy road. After a few minutes she realized that they seemed to be climbing. "Is Copper Canyon in the mountains?" she asked.

"It's a little over four thousand feet," he said, "but it's more rolling hills than jagged peaks. Don't be afraid. We're not in any danger of going over a cliff. All we have to worry about is if the snow will get too high for this four-wheel-drive vehicle to get through, but it's high off the ground and has snow tires so we'll be okay. There are some tapes in the glove compartment if you'd like to play one."

She chose a cassette and put it in the player, hoping it would take her mind off the storm. "How much farther do we have to go?"

Jim's hands clenched the steering wheel and he bent forward and kept his gaze straight ahead in an effort to see through the gathering darkness and the thick snow. "It's ten miles from Grangeville to Copper Canyon, and the farm's about four miles out of town. Don't worry, I could drive this road in my sleep."

Yes, but can he drive it in a blinding snowstorm? She decided he could do it better if she didn't pester him with questions and settled back to listen to the music.

It seemed like forever before Jim announced they were approaching Copper Canyon, although Coralie didn't know how he could tell. All she could see was darkness and swirling snow.

At one point he turned left, and then she saw the faint twinkling of lights through the haze. "How big is this town?" she asked, wishing she could see it better.

"The population's approximately three thousand, give or take a few," he answered. "It's a pretty place with lots of trees and well-kept homes. It's primarily a farming community, but it gets a fair amount of year-round tourist trade with Hell's Canyon in one direction and great skiing in the other."

"I wish I could see it," she said wistfully.

He chuckled. "You will, I promise. Just as soon as the weather and the roads clear."

There was no traffic, and after a few more blocks she didn't see any more lights.

"The driveway that leads to the house is on your side of the road," Jim said. "You can help me watch for the mailbox. It should show up in the headlights, but it's difficult for me to see from this side of the Cherokee."

She could believe that. It was difficult for her to see and she was on the closer side. A few minutes later, though, she caught sight of a mound of snow that could be a rural mailbox. "Is that it?" she asked and pointed just before he turned off the road and headed up the driveway.

"That was it," he confirmed. "We're home."

Her relief was monumental, and she let out the breath she'd more or less been holding all the way from Grangeville. "Thank you, God," she murmured softly.

The house was set quite away back from the road, and she couldn't see it until the headlights picked it up. Even then it was more shadow and outline than substance.

Jim pulled around to the back of the building and stopped. This area was well lighted, and Coralie could see that the house had a high foundation with several steps leading to a screened-in porch. Whoever had built it was obviously well aware of the inordinate amount of snow the winter blizzards dumped on this part of Idaho.

"Don't try to get out until I come around and get you," Jim said as he opened the door without turning off the motor and the lights.

In seconds he opened the door on her side and reached out to put one arm under her knees and the other around her back. She shied away. "You needn't carry me, I can walk."

He glanced at her feet. "In those flimsy little shoes? This snow would be knee-deep on you. You'd ruin your shoes and freeze your feet and legs. Now hurry up and put your arms around my neck. I've got to put the Cherokee in the garage before the snow drifts any more, or I won't be able to open the door."

She immediately stopped arguing and did as he asked. If his story was true, and she had no reason to doubt it, then he was being extraordinarily considerate of her. It was about time she stopped being a hindrance and started trying to help.

He carried her up the steps, through the porch and into the brightly lit rustic kitchen where they were greeted by two young girls and an older man who had apparently heard them coming.

"Holy mackerel, Jimmy, where'd you get her?" asked the man, who was obviously Jim's father.

"This is Coralie Dixon, Dad," he said and stood her down on the floor. "I'll introduce you all and explain later, but first I have to take care of the Cherokee. Be right back." He turned and went back out the door, slamming it shut behind him.

Coralie was left alone with Jim's family, and for the first time in her life she couldn't think of anything to say. Apparently, neither could they because the silence was uncomfortable and embarrassing, but the mouth-watering aroma of roast beef and fresh-perked coffee almost overcame it.

Finally Buck spoke. "I . . . I'm Jim's dad, Buck. Please, let me take your coat, Miss Dixon. I'll bet you're hungry. Supper's ready anytime you and Jim are."

This man would never be a poker player. His face was flushed with guilt, and he looked everywhere but at her as she took off her coat and handed it to him. He took it, then held it out to the girls. "Here, you two take this and hang it up in the closet.

The younger daughter, Amber, took it and turned to leave, but the elder one, Gloria, wasn't as easily ordered around. "I want to stay here."

Buck glared at her. "Go into the other room with your sister," he commanded. "We'll all talk when your dad gets here."

Gloria sulked, but followed Amber out of sight.

Coralie caught Buck's gaze and speared it with her own. He looked like a nice old guy with a sort of shy, cherubic expression, but she wasn't going to let him off the hook easily.

"Shame on you, Mr. Buckley," she said softly.

Color flooded his face and he looked down at his feet. "Aw, gee, ma'am, I'm sorry. I was only tryin' to help Jim find a wife. He'll probably never get around to lookin' for one on his own after the way Marsha ran out on him."

He raised his head then and studied her. "Are you sure you're Coralie Dixon? You're so much younger . . ."

Now it was her turn to blush. He was right. She was as guilty of deception as he was. She might as well confess. "I'm twenty-two. That was a picture of my aunt that I sent."

A smile lit Buck's wrinkled face. "Does Jim know that?"

She nodded. "Sure. He spotted the discrepancy right away."

Buck's smile widened. "And he brought you home, anyway? That's great. He left here this morning vowing to send you back to California."

It was no use, she couldn't possibly hold a grudge against this guileless man who's only fault was wanting his son to be happy, and confusing Jim's goals with his own.

Reluctantly, she shook her head. "He tried to send me back, but there wasn't another flight out today and they were preparing to shut down the airport because of the blizzard. He only brought me back here with him because he thought I was too young to take care of myself until the storm's over. I'll be leaving, though, as soon as the roads—"

The rest of her sentence was drowned out by the sound of Jim stamping the snow off his boots on the porch just before he opened the door and came in carrying her suitcase.

The girls heard him, too, and came running from the other part of the house, both of them talking at once and vying for his attention. "Dad, who's that lady?" "Where did you get her?" "Why did you bring her here?"

Jim put the suitcase down on the floor and held up his hand for silence. "Now hold on. I told you I'd introduce you and I will, but let me get my coat off first."

He shrugged out of his jacket and hung it on the wall rack beside the door, then hung his hat next to it. He put an arm around each girl and the three of them turned to face Coralie and Buck. "Coralie," he said, "I'd like you to meet my daughters, Gloria and Amber." He nodded to each one as he spoke, then looked at Buck. "And you remember that sly old man with the guilty look. You can call him Grandpa."

Coralie almost choked on a suppressed giggle. He probably was about the same age as her grandpa at that, but she knew Jim was not so subtly rubbing the age difference in to both of them.

"We introduced ourselves again," she murmured.

"I'll just bet you did," he said with a knowing lift of his eyebrow, then continued his introduction. "Girls, this lady is Coralie Dixon, from Eureka, California. She's a friend of your grandfather's."

Buck uttered a short yip of surprise and protest before he managed to get it under control, but he recovered quickly. "She sure is," he said with a straight face. "Known her since she was a baby."

He closed his mouth and looked at Jim as if to say, Okay, now the ball's in your court again.

Coralie was glad she and Jim had plotted this little story in advance or it could have turned into a real donnybrook. She also decided she'd better take control of it before the whole thing got completely out of hand.

Chapter Four

"I'm very glad to meet you," Coralie said to the girls, "and it's really great to see you again, Uncle Buck."

Buck blinked his surprise as Amber, the pretty little blond daughter, voiced hers. "Grandpa's your uncle?"

"Well, not really," Coralie backtracked. "But when I was a little girl he and my dad were close friends, and he said I could call him Uncle Buck."

"Did you live in Copper Canyon?" Gloria asked suspiciously. "I don't remember any Dixons—"

"No. That is I . . ." Coralie stammered. Damn, she never had been any good at lying. "My . . . my dad and your grandpa were good buddies in the army during the Korean War, and afterward they stayed in close touch even though my parents live in a small town in the northern panhandle of the state. I live in California now."

"How come?" Amber interrupted.

"Be-because that . . . that's where I work," she improvised, caught off guard by the question.

"What kind of work do you do?" Gloria again.

"I'm a medical assistant." Coralie was relieved that she could tell the truth for a change. "I'm trained to assist both nurses and laboratory technicians in hospitals or clinics. Right now I'm working in the lab at the hospital in Eureka, a town in northern California."

"Then how did you and dad get together today?" Gloria asked.

"She'd been visiting her parents," Jim said, picking up the story they'd plotted, "and was scheduled to catch a flight back to California this morning, but it was canceled because of the winter storm warning. She called here to invite Grandpa to come to Lewiston and spend the afternoon with her since they hadn't seen each other for several years. He'd gone into town, though, and I didn't know where to reach him so I told her I'd come instead."

Coralie was more than happy to let him continue.

"By the time I got to the airport all flights had been canceled because of the blizzard. They were shutting down and expected to be closed for a couple of days. Naturally, I didn't want to leave Coralie there all alone so I talked her into coming home with me."

At this point Buck jumped in and added his own touch to the fiction. "In that case I'm real happy for the blizzard," he said with a glowing smile. "Little Coralie Dixon. You're all grown up. Come here and give your old Uncle Buck a big hug."

They embraced, and Buck whispered in her ear, "Looks like we're all guilty of a little creative storytellin', don't it?"

She was quite sure she blushed. "Not bad for spur of the moment, though," she whispered back.

Buck hooted with laughter and released her. "You're shivering with cold," he said. "Why don't you go upstairs and take a hot shower before we eat. Can't have you gettin' sick. Jim'll show you to your room."

"We don't have any extra bedrooms," Gloria said. "Grandpa's staying over and I'm not giving up mine."

"Me, either," Amber chimed in.

Coralie was surprised by their rudeness, and she could feel the tension building in the room.

"No problem," Buck said quickly. "I'll just go on home after dinner. I got plenty of food and stuff to last out the storm—"

"No, you won't," Jim interrupted. "You're not staying in that house alone during a blizzard. You'll keep the spare room, and Amber can move in with Gloria."

"No way!" the girls chimed in chorus.

They continued to protest and argue loudly with Jim and each other while Coralie stood by feeling like an interloper. If Jim didn't have room for her why had he insisted she come home with him? He could have taken her to a hotel in Lewiston and left her there.

Unfortunately, there was no way out of this unpleasant situation. It was too dangerous to try to drive in this storm, and besides, the roads were probably closed by now. All she really wanted was that shower Buck had offered and a place to curl up and go to sleep.

She glanced at Buck and saw that he looked embarrassed, too. "I'm sorry it's so inconvenient having me here," she said.

He frowned and opened his mouth to say something, but she hurried on. "I'd never have come if I'd known, but I don't need a whole room. Surely there must be a couch somewhere in this house. I can sleep on it."

Buck shook his head. "I won't hear of it," he said, then raised his arms and clapped his hands together with a bang that immediately got the attention of his son and granddaughters.

"Shut up and listen to me," he demanded. "I'm ashamed of all three of you. You've embarrassed my guest, and I'm not going to stand for that. She can have the spare bedroom, I'm going home to my own house."

Jim and the girls were too shocked by his outburst to respond immediately, but then Jim spoke. He didn't raise his voice, but the force behind it was commanding. "No, Dad, you aren't. I'm not going to let you ride out this storm alone in that house where I won't be able to get to you."

He looked at Coralie, and she saw the shame and remorse in his expression. "Coralie, I'm so sorry," he said huskily, then turned and glared at his daughters.

"Not one more word," he warned them, and his tone brooked no arguing. "Go upstairs and do as I told you. Right now!"

The startled girls looked at him, then at each other, then turned and fled out of the room and up the stairs, the sound of their flying footsteps broadcasting their pace.

Jim turned once more to face Coralie and Buck. "I'm sorry," he said again, his whole demeanor mirroring his deeply felt regret. "I promise there won't be any more scenes like this. Coralie can take Amber's bedroom. The girls are upstairs moving her things into Gloria's room and making up the bed with clean sheets. Gloria has twin beds and plenty of space. Both kids will be comfortable."

He focused on Coralie. "I apologize for my daughters. I'm afraid they're altogether too used to having their own way. I often fall far short of being the ideal father. I still have a lot to learn."

It was obvious that he meant everything he said, and her instinct was to forgive him and relieve him of his guilt, but she knew it wasn't that simple. His daughters were apparently spoiled brats, and she didn't care for them. That meant she'd better not get too involved with their father because they came as a package.

It was a good thing she and Jim had already agreed that neither of them was interested in a mail order marriage partner.

"I'm sorry, too," she said coolly. "You needn't have invited me to wait out the storm here with your family. I never would have come if I'd known my presence was going to be such a nuisance."

He shook his head. "No, it's not a nuisance. You mustn't take Amber and Gloria's squabbling personally."

Coralie wasn't sure how he expected her to accomplish that, but she saw no point in arguing the matter. Besides, she was exhausted and her feet were wet and cold. "In that case if you don't mind I'd like to take a hot shower and go to bed."

Jim frowned. "But surely you'll have supper first."

She shook her head. "Thank you, but I'm not hungry, and I've been up since four-thirty this morning. I really need some rest."

Jim looked at her and cursed himself for an oaf. There were deep lines of weariness around her mouth, and the dark shadows under her lovely eyes stood out against her white face. Unable to stop himself he reached out and stroked her damp, windblown hair. "You do look tired," he murmured and picked up her suitcase. "Come on, I'll show you to your room."

There were three bedrooms and two bathrooms upstairs, one bath at the end of the hall and the other off the master bedroom where Jim slept. He explained the layout to her and led her into the room across the hall from his. It was a typical adolescent girls hideaway decorated with pink chintz spread and curtains, stuffed animals and posters of pop music stars on the walls. He was embarrassed to see that it was also messy as usual with dirty clothes and soft drink cans still lying where they'd been tossed.

"Sorry about the mess," he mumbled as he put the suitcase on the bed and started gathering things up.

"I thought there were four bedrooms," she commented, ignoring his apology.

"There are," Jim said. "The fourth one is downstairs off the kitchen. That's where Dad sleeps when he stays here.

The only shower up here is in the master bath. I'll put clean towels in there for you."

She looked startled. "Oh, but I don't need a shower," she hastened to assure him. "I can take a bath in the one at the end of the hall. I don't want to bother you, too."

She bothered him all right, but not the way she meant. It was going to be difficult to think of her as just another one of the kids while they were snowbound in such small quarters.

He managed a grin. "You won't bother me," he assured her. "Not unless you decide to shower at three o'clock in the morning. Now that might just possibly be a distraction."

And that was the understatement of the year. If he found her in his shower in the middle of the night she'd be a distraction he wouldn't be able to resist!

"I'll try to remember that," she teased with an answering grin.

Coralie woke at eight o'clock the following morning to dark clouds, howling wind and swirling snow. The blizzard had apparently been raging all night, but she hadn't heard a thing since tumbling into the soft warm bed immediately after taking a steaming hot, relaxing shower.

The wind shook the house, and she snuggled under the down-filled quilt and started to doze off again, but the tantalizing aroma of bacon and fresh-perked coffee beckoned from downstairs. She hadn't had bacon and eggs for breakfast since moving out of her parents' home. A cup of instant coffee, a glass of orange juice and a piece of toast was all she ever had time for before rushing off to work. Besides, she had to watch her weight, and eating fried eggs and bacon was definitely not the way to do it.

This morning, though, she was going to make an exception. Pangs of hunger reminded her that she hadn't eaten since lunch the day before. She threw back the heavy covers and climbed out of bed, then immediately wished she was back in it. Even through the flannel nightie she'd had the good sense to bring she felt the chill in the room, and the polished hardwood floor under her bare feet was cold.

Quickly, she rummaged through her suitcase and dressed in blue jeans and a heavy royal blue sweatshirt. The thick socks she wore under her boots helped to warm her feet. Grabbing her zippered cosmetic case, she headed for the bathroom.

Half an hour later, after straightening up her room and unpacking her clothes, Coralie went downstairs and followed the mouth-watering smells into the kitchen. It was empty except for Buck, who was doing something at the sink.

He looked up when she appeared, and his expressive face lit with a big smile. "Well, hi there. You're lookin' pert 'n' pretty this mornin'. Did you sleep okay?"

She smiled back. "Yes, thanks. I didn't hear a thing from the time I crawled into the bed until I woke up about half an hour ago." She looked around. "Where is everybody? Am I early or late?"

He reached for a towel and dried his hands. "Neither. Jim and I get up at five o'clock every day, but the girls sleep most of the mornin' when they don't have to get up. Today there's no school because of the storm so they're still in bed, and Jim's out doin' the chores. He should be back any minute."

He put down the towel and nodded toward the round walnut table. "Sit down and have a cup of coffee while I fix your breakfast. Do you like pancakes with your bacon and eggs?"

"Let me do that," she said as she walked over to the big old iron stove. "I'm perfectly capable of cooking my own breakfast."

"That's not necessary," he protested. "I'm pretty much chief cook and bottle washer around here until Jim finds a new housekeeper."

She detoured to the refrigerator, opened the door and took out a bowl of extra large fresh eggs and a package of bacon. "Then it's time you had a little help."

She carried the items to the counter and peeled off two pieces of bacon. "Can I fix some for you, too?"

He shook his head. "Naw, I already ate, but—"

"May I use that skillet," she interrupted before he could protest again, and nodded at the cast-iron frying pan sitting at the back of the stove.

"Yeah, sure," he said and pulled it over onto a front burner, then turned on the flame, "but I wish you'd let me do it. You're our guest."

She put the bacon in the skillet. "No, Buck, I'm not a guest. I'm a stranger who is imposing on your hospitality until the roads are open again, and I won't have you waiting on me."

"Darn it, Coralie, it don't matter what you and Jim told the girls, I got you into this by sendin' for you and that makes you my guest. Besides, I'd be pleased to wait on you."

She turned the bacon and picked up an egg. "I came here of my own accord," she reminded him, "and I'd be pleased to help you. How about if we work together? You can do the cooking and I'll do the cleaning."

He chuckled. "If that idiot son of mine doesn't know a treasure when he finds one, would you consider me as second choice?" His eyes sparkled with mischief.

She giggled like a schoolgirl and broke the egg in the pan with the bacon. "If I wanted to get married you'd be my *first* choice," she told him teasingly. "Jim's too old and set in his ways for me."

Buck howled with laughter just as the door opened and Jim came stomping in. He looked up and saw Coralie and his dad beaming with high spirits. The joyful sound of their easy friendship brought a stab of chagrin to his midsection. "What's so funny?" he asked, and his tone betrayed his... his what? Hurt? Jealousy?

That thought brought him up short. What in hell was the matter with him? Jealousy! That was ridiculous. He didn't even know the woman. So why was he disgruntled to find her laughing with his father after she'd been so cool and distant with him most of the time last night?

Buck had probably earned her laughter, just as Jim knew he'd earned her displeasure the night before. He'd allowed his children to humiliate her, and she had a right to be upset.

"Coralie just offered to help with the cooking and housework while she's here," Buck explained gleefully, "and I asked her to marry me. She's thinking about it," he finished slyly.

Jim wasn't amused. "Oh, for..." Something caught his attention and he sniffed. "What's burning?"

Both Coralie and Buck gasped and turned to the stove. Jim saw what was going to happen, but didn't have time to stop it or even shout a warning as Coralie reached for the iron handle of the skillet and grabbed it.

It was hot, and with a shrill cry she pulled back and clutched her hand with the other one.

"Oh, my God!" Jim moaned, feeling her pain as if it were his own. Quickly, he turned off the burner, then caught her around her waist and hurried her to the sink. He turned on the cold water and held her hand under it. "Just keep it there," he instructed, then picked up a large bowl from the counter and hurried out into the roaring blizzard. He scooped the bowl full of snow and took it back in.

Coming up behind her he put the dish back on the counter, then guided her hand into it. "Here now, this'll make it feel better," he said, and turned to call over his shoulder. "Dad, bring me the aloe vera cream from the medicine cabinet in the bathroom! Quick!"

He returned his attention to Coralie. Her back was cradled against his chest, and his left arm was still around her waist as he covered the back of her right hand with his to keep it in the snow.

She was shivering in his arms, but he didn't know whether it was from the pain or the cold. Probably both. His arm tightened around her and he rubbed his cheek against her temple. "I'm so sorry, honey. Are you all right?" he murmured in her ear.

A wave of relief swept over him as she snuggled into his embrace instead of pulling away from him as he'd feared she would. "I'm fine," she assured him. "It's my own fault. I should have known better than to touch that handle without a hot pad."

The sound of footsteps broke the all-too-brief spell, and he assumed it was Buck returning until a sharp gasp and Gloria's voice rang through the room. "Dad! What's going on? Why are you making out with *her?*"

Too startled to think, let alone reason, Jim jumped away from Coralie and spun around to face his elder daughter, making himself look guilty as charged.

"Gloria! Where did you come from? What are you doing here?"

Oh, great! So much for his expertise in dealing with teenage daughters. He sounded like a fifteen-year-old himself who'd just been caught in the haystack with his girlfriend.

Gloria's cheeks were red, and she made no effort to lower her voice. "What am *I* doing here!" she said indignantly. "I live in this house, and I came down to get some breakfast. What are *you* doing with *her?*"

It was the disdainful way she spoke about Coralie that finally reminded him who and where he was. "I live here, too, young lady, and in case you've forgotten I own the house and I'm the one who's in charge."

She blinked and looked surprised, which she probably was since he'd never talked to her that way before.

Jim was aware that Buck had come back into the room, but he was too worked up to care about privacy. "Ms. Dixon burned her hand on the hot skillet," he continued, "and I was keeping snow on it while Grandpa went for the aloe vera."

He reached out to Buck. "Give it to me, Dad," he said, and Buck handed it to him, then went back to cooking breakfast for those who hadn't eaten yet.

"But...but it looked like you had your arms around her," a somewhat subdued Gloria said.

"I did have one arm around her," he admitted tersely. "She was in a lot of pain, and I was holding her steady while I put her other hand in the bowl of snow. Now you owe both Ms. Dixon and me an apology, and I want to hear it."

Gloria looked as if she were going to protest, but apparently thought better of it. Instead, she raised her head, and her expression was one of defiance. "I'm sorry," she said crisply, and for the first time in her young life he saw hostility directed toward him in her wide brown eyes.

Jim's heart melted at his child's discomfort, but she had to learn that rudeness was not acceptable. He knew he should deal with his daughter's incipient rebellion right now, but Coralie's hand needed attention that couldn't wait. "You're forgiven," he said, "but next time think before you speak."

Gloria didn't answer, but turned on her heel and stormed out of the room.

Jim turned to Coralie, who now had her back to the counter and held the bowl of snow in one hand as she soaked the other one in it. "Again I apologize for my daughter," he said anxiously. "I don't know what's gotten into her. She's not usually this obnoxious."

He knew that wasn't altogether true. Both Gloria and Amber could be sweet as angels when they were getting their own way, but they were also little devils when crossed. Particularly Gloria, but Amber tended to follow her lead. He gave in to them a lot of the time just to keep them happy.

Coralie wasn't inclined to bet on the truth of Jim's last statement. She suspected that he knew he'd spoiled them, but just didn't want to admit it. She wondered if their mother overindulged them, too. Well, there was no sense in making an issue of it. She'd only be here a day or two.

"Fourteen's a difficult age," she told him. "Gloria's jealous of me. She doesn't want to share you, especially not with another woman."

Jim had picked up a soft towel and was gently patting her burned hand dry. His own hands were big and callused, but he handled hers so tenderly that she could almost ignore the pain.

At her words he raised his head and looked at her, his eyes round with disbelief. "Gloria jealous? That's nonsense. She's just a little girl."

Coralie cringed as he unintentionally rubbed her palm harder than he'd intended. "No, she's not, Jim," she countered, "but even if she were it wouldn't make any difference. Little girls are as apt to be possessive of their fathers as older ones are. We all want our parents' undivided attention, and even more so in a one-parent household."

"What makes you such an expert on the subject?" Jim grumbled. "You're not much more than a child yourself."

She winced. There it was, that damned age difference again. Apparently, he was never going to give in and admit that she was old enough to vote. "Maybe that's what makes me an expert," she said with a sigh. "I'm still young enough to remember the feelings I had as a child."

"Were you ever jealous of your father?" he asked.

She hesitated, unwilling to open that can of worms. Unfortunately, though, she'd already done so, which left her no choice but to answer the question. "As a matter of fact I was, and still am," she said. "My mother died when I was ten, and my dad kind of relied on me to take charge of my little sister and brother. We had part-time help, but I was 'Daddy's big girl.' His helper. I got possessive, too, just like Gloria, and when Dad started bringing home the woman who is now my stepmother you better believe I was jealous.''

Jim's expression changed from argumentative to repentant, and he caressed her wrist with his finger. "Oh, hey,'' he said, "I'm sorry. I didn't know...''

"Of course you didn't,'' she answered gently. "I don't talk about my selfishness. For a long time I wouldn't even admit it to myself. I blamed my stepmother instead, but she is a wise and patient woman, a school counselor, who worked patiently with me to make me see that she wasn't going to take my daddy or my brother and sister away from me. She just wanted to be a part of our lives and take over as woman of the house so I could be a carefree child again.''

Jim was liberally applying aloe vera cream to her burns. "And did she succeed?''

The cool cream felt good on her hot palm and fingers, and the love she felt for her second mother welled up inside her. "Oh, yes, and I'll be forever grateful to her. I love her dearly, but—''

She snapped her mouth shut and wished she'd done it one word sooner.

Jim raised one eyebrow. "But?''

She might as well finish the sentence. After all, it was the point she was trying to make. "But sometimes when I'm with them and Dad is being affectionate with her, I feel left out and a twinge of the old jealousy comes back.''

Jim pondered that for a moment. "But Gloria isn't the woman of the house—''

"Yes, she is,'' Coralie interrupted. "Since her mother no longer lives with you Gloria is the oldest female in your family. The unofficial 'hostess.' The 'woman in charge,' so to speak. I'll bet you rely on her to baby-sit her younger sister when there's not another adult around. Or to start supper when neither you nor Buck are able to do it."

"Well...yes, but she's just a kid," he insisted.

"She's a young woman," Coralie contradicted, "and Amber's not far behind. Don't you ever look at them? Gloria is stunning. That rich dark brown hair fairly shimmers around her shoulders, and those long thick eyelashes draw attention to her beautiful wide brown eyes."

Jim still held Coralie's hand, but he'd obviously forgotten about it. He was too busy staring at her in utter amazement. "Well, sure, she's pretty, but..."

His voice trailed off as if he were thinking of what she'd said and didn't like the conclusion he was drawing.

She couldn't help but smile. "You better wake up and smell the coffee, Daddy," she teased. "By the end of the year you're going to have to chase the boys away with a stick."

Jim groaned. "Oh, God, I hope not. I'm not ready for that yet."

This time she laughed. "No father ever is," she told him gleefully. "I advise you to marry the next woman who answers your ad in that magazine. You're going to need help!"

The rest of the day was uneventful; in fact, it was downright boring once she'd learned the layout of the ground floor of the house. It consisted of a big comfortable living room, a dining room, the oversize kitchen, which was the warmest room in the building and therefore the one Coralie gravitated to most, the spare bedroom and a bathroom with both a tub and a shower.

The storm continued unabated and the temperature plummeted to below zero. She was afraid to ask what the windchill factor was. Although the house was well built and the windows were double paned, the extreme cold and high winds still made it hard to heat, and Coralie pulled on a heavy sweater over her sweatshirt.

The weather conditions made television and radio reception so poor that it was too annoying to try to watch or listen to them, so everyone was left at loose ends. Jim retreated to his bedroom, which also served as an office, to catch up on his paperwork. The girls whined about the lack of television until they finally settled down at the dining room table with a giant jigsaw puzzle, and Coralie fidgeted.

Buck managed to keep busy in the kitchen what with cooking and cleaning up after three meals. She tried to assist him, but because of her burned hand she was more of a hindrance than a help. Jim had coated it with the soothing cream and then covered it with a thin layer of gauze so that she wouldn't get the medication on everything she touched, but even so it was stiff and sore and useless.

Toward midafternoon she finally decided to try to get better acquainted with Gloria and Amber and wandered into the dining room. "Do you mind if I join you?" she asked.

Amber looked at Gloria, and Gloria shrugged. "If you want to," she said without looking up.

Well, at least she hadn't said no. Coralie sat down at the end of the table, which put her between the two girls. "Is this puzzle new, or have you put it together before?" she asked as she examined the picture on the box top.

She was surprised to see that it was an incredibly complicated one. The inside of an ancient Greek art gallery, the walls lined with paintings and a large number of people dressed in the costumes of the day milling around or sitting and reclining on the furniture. The blurb claimed that the puzzle contained eight thousand pieces.

"Our mother gave it to us for Christmas," Amber said, "and we tried to put it together once, but it was too hard."

Well, of course it was, unless they were champion puzzle solvers, Coralie thought impatiently. The pieces were too small, and there were so many colors, figures and jumbled background decorations in the painting that it would be extremely difficult for an adult to assemble it. Not only that, but it was much too gaudy to be pretty. It certainly wasn't appropriate for children, or even young teenagers.

"Do you two work a lot of jigsaw puzzles," she asked.

Gloria shook her head. "No. Almost never. We have one or two around here someplace, but I haven't seen them in years."

What had their mother been thinking of? Coralie thought. Surely she knew her daughters well enough to realize they were too young and inexperienced to sort out a jigsaw puzzle of this magnitude.

"You're right, it is hard," she said reassuringly. "I don't think I can put it all together, either, but maybe with the three of us working on it we can get a good start. Did your mother have any luck with it?"

"Our mother doesn't live with us," Gloria interjected.

"We haven't seen her for more than two years," Amber explained, as if she owed Coralie a clarification.

Coralie tried not to let her shock show. She knew Jim was divorced, but she hadn't realized that his ex-wife didn't share in the custody of their children.

"Oh, I see," she said carefully. "Then I guess we'll have to just bumble through this puzzle and see how far we get."

She was intensely curious about Jim's wife, and his marriage and divorce, but she knew better than to pry. She'd just have to wait and glean whatever information she could from tidbits dropped here and there in table talk. Not that it was any of her business, she silently reminded herself.

The afternoon went by more quickly after that, and by dinnertime—supper time as they called it—they'd made quite a bit of progress. Coralie had gained some headway with Jim's children, too. Not a lot, but enough to be encouraging. Amber was friendlier than Gloria, but even Gloria unbent enough to initiate short conversations with Coralie now and then as they wrestled with trying to fit round pieces into square holes.

When she smelled chicken frying Coralie realized that Buck was fixing supper. She wondered why the girls hadn't been called to help, and she was just about to excuse herself and go in the kitchen to offer to when Jim walked into the dining room.

He stopped short and looked at the three people sitting around the table peacefully putting a puzzle together. A relieved smile lit his handsome face.

Then he made another blunder.

Chapter Five

"So here you are," Jim said happily. "It's been so quiet around here that I've been wondering where the three of you were. I'm glad to see that all my girls are getting along and have found a way to entertain yourselves."

"Coralie's *not* one of your girls," Gloria snarled as she stood and pushed back her chair. "She's too old to be our sister and she's too young to be your girlfriend. Besides, fathers don't have girlfriends."

He watched, dumbfounded, as his daughter rushed out of the room. What in hell had brought that on?

Glancing at Amber and Coralie, who looked equally shocked, he knew he was going to have to deal with this situation immediately, but how? Why had Gloria turned into such a little hellion lately? She didn't used to be that way. It was only since her mother left that . . .

He groaned and ran his fingers through his hair. That's when everything had fallen apart, and he had no idea how to make it right again.

"I . . . I'm sorry," he said to Coralie for what must have been about the hundredth time since he'd carried her into the house. "What did I say wrong? I wasn't scolding her."

Coralie seemed equally at a loss. "I'm not sure. She and I have been getting along pretty well this afternoon. We've been working on this puzzle and there was no unpleasantness . . ."

Her voice trailed off, and he turned to look at Amber. She looked stricken and tears brimmed in her eyes. As usual he melted at his child's tears and walked over to hunker down beside her. "It's all right, baby," he said soothingly. "Don't cry. Do you know why she blew up like that?"

One tear fell and ran down her cheek. "Sh-she doesn't want Coralie here. Neither do I. If she stays around you'll probably marry her, and then you won't want us anymore."

His heart ached for the child as he gathered her in his arms. "Your sister's mistaken," he said tenderly. "I never saw Coralie until yesterday, and she'll only be here until the storm is over. Then she's going back to her home in California. What makes you think I'm going to marry her?"

Amber hiccuped. "Gloria said—"

"Ah, yes, 'Gloria said.' I think we'd better go upstairs and have a talk with that young lady."

Amber shook her head against his chest. "No," she said vehemently. "Don't bawl her out."

Jim sighed with regret. About the only times he could remember having bawled Gloria out were the two times—one last night and one this morning—when she'd been blatantly disrespectful to Coralie, but now both of his girls thought of him as an ogre. He couldn't win for losing!

He stroked Amber's soft blond hair that was so much like her mother's. "I'm not going to scold her," he promised. "I just think the three of us need to talk things out. Obviously you've both got some wrong ideas about what's going on."

He released her and stood, intending to ask Coralie to excuse them, but her chair was empty. Damn! Had he said something to offend *her* now? He didn't seem able to please women of any age anymore.

Coralie was setting the table in the kitchen when she heard Jim and Amber go upstairs. The steps were uncarpeted as were all the floors except in the living and dining rooms, so it was easy to keep track of where people were in the house by listening to the footsteps.

She felt unwanted and depressed. It seemed that she caused trouble in the Buckley family no matter what she did. She'd be so glad when this storm was over and she could go home.

The problem was that she no longer had a home. She'd burned all her bridges behind her. Although there had been no commitment with Jim—or as it turned out with Buck acting for Jim—on the mail order bride thing, she'd been determined not to go back to California.

The whole blasted state seemed to be forever shaken by disastrous earthquakes, and she wasn't going back to be maimed or killed by one of them. So she'd quit her job at the hospital, sold her car and packed up the rest of her belongings for Kirsten to send on to her. Either here in Copper Canyon if she and Jim had hit it off and gotten married, or wherever she finally decided to settle.

She hadn't told Jim all this and it was a good thing. She didn't want him feeling any more responsible for her than he already did. As far as he knew she was going back to a home, friends and family in California.

"Coralie, could you hand me that platter on the top shelf of the cupboard over there," Buck called from his place at the stove. "Gotta take the chicken out of this skillet so's I can make the gravy in it."

"Sure," she said and opened the cupboard door. The top shelf was high and she had to stand on her toes to reach it. Without thinking she grabbed for the platter with her right hand—the one that was burned—and the contact sent a sharp shaft of pain down her arm. Her hand opened involuntarily and the platter dropped to the tile counter with a loud crash and broke.

"Damn! Damn! Damn!" she raged as Buck came running.

"Did you hurt yourself?" he asked anxiously as he looked at the pieces of broken pottery all over the counter.

"No, I'm not hurt," she said bitterly, "but I'm totally useless. I can't do anything right. All I'm good at is causing trouble!"

She was sobbing, and stupid tears streamed down her cheeks, which was just one more flaw. Strong, competent women never cry!

Buck put his arm around her and led her to a chair, then sat her down. "There now, don't feel so bad. That old platter isn't gonna be missed—we'll use another one. And don't go blamin' yourself for all the upheaval that's been goin' on around here. It's not your fault. You're just the—what's the word?—um, *catalyst*. That's it."

He crossed the room and turned off the burner under the skillet, then returned to sit down beside her.

"There's been a whole lot of rage, and guilt, and grief bubblin' under the surface in all of us since Marsha left," he said, "but none of us has been willing to voice it. I couldn't vent my spleen to Jim because he'd feel he had to defend her. He couldn't criticize her to his daughters 'cause she was their mother and he didn't want them to think badly of her. And they were too crushed by her goin' off like that to talk about it to anybody. Then, too, I guess we all felt guilty for not facing the fact that she was so unhappy and doin' somethin' about it."

Coralie was so surprised by Buck's unexpected revelation that she forgot her own anguish. "Marsha was Jim's wife?" she asked, wanting to make sure she hadn't misunderstood anything.

Buck sighed. "Yeah. They'd been married thirteen years when she just packed her bags one day while the kids were in school and Jim was out in the fields and disappeared without even sayin' goodbye. She left a note tellin' him she was goin' to the city and never wanted to see the farm again."

Coralie was astounded. Surely there was something Buck didn't know about the situation, or wasn't telling her. It was hard enough to believe that any woman would leave Jim, unless there was a side to him that she hadn't seen yet, but to abandon her children? No! If she did she must have had a good reason.

"But why?" The question exploded from her. "What city? Where did she go?"

Buck shrugged. "I never did understand why, except that she and Jim never seemed to be really happy. She complained a lot, and she made no secret of the fact that she hated farm life, but she was a pretty good mother.

"As for where she went, she didn't say what city and it took Jim several months to track her down. He finally found her in Denver. She was working as a waitress and had an apartment and a new man. She told Jim she was filing for divorce and he could have full custody of the kids."

Coralie was still stunned. How could any woman voluntarily give up her children? Such a thing was unthinkable. "But surely she sees them now and then? Talks to them on the phone?"

Buck shook his head sadly. "She hasn't seen or talked to them since she left. The only time she gets in touch is Christmas and birthdays. She sends them presents at Christmas and cards on their birthdays."

The woman must be out of her mind, Coralie thought.

"I know Jimmy isn't strict enough with the kids," Buck continued. "They're both spoiled rotten, but he can't forget how they cried themselves to sleep over their mother every night after she left. He knows they feel abandoned and forgotten. That's why he can't bring himself to say no to them, or make them help around the house. They think their mother sort of threw them away, and he can't bear to have them think he doesn't love them, either.''

Coralie was touched by Jim's devotion to his children. She hoped that someday they'd fully realize how fortunate they were to have him for a father. Overindulging them wasn't the best way for him to show his love, but no parent was perfect.

Now that she understood their behavior better she vowed to try harder to like them and help them if she could.

Buck shifted restlessly in his chair and stood. ''Well, now that I've spilled all the family secrets I better get back to my cookin'. Why don't you go wash the tear tracks off your cheeks and then call Jim and the kids to come down for supper before it gets cold.''

Coralie went to bed early that night since there wasn't anything else to do. The storm continued to rage, there was no television, radio or newspaper, and the only place she could keep really warm was between the feather mattress and the down comforter in Amber's bed.

She slept for a while until a loud crackling noise outside her window woke her. It startled her, but then she realized it was probably another tree branch wrenched off the trunk by the wind. That had happened several times today.

She snuggled down again and closed her eyes, but now sleep eluded her. The continuous howl of the wind chipped at her nerves until they were raw. She'd never been in a blizzard before, and she'd had no idea they could last so long.

She was beginning to wonder if this storm would ever end. How much longer could it snow before it piled up so high that they couldn't get out of the house? Would they have enough gas to heat with? What if the electricity went off and they had no lights? How could Jim and Buck feed the animals if they couldn't get to the barn?

She tossed, and turned, and tried to think of something pleasant, but the few times she got her mind off the storm it immediately focused on Jim and his unhappy marriage and divorce. Why had his wife left him and their children? What kind of woman was she? Had Jim loved her and been heartbroken when she ran away? Did he still miss her and want her?

A loud bang from outside brought her straight up in bed, hugging the quilt to her. Good heavens, what was that! It didn't sound like a tree branch—it was metallic.

She was shivering, but it was more with nerves than with cold. She couldn't stay upstairs in the dark listening to the storm any longer. Throwing back the covers she turned on the lamp, then reached for the purple velour robe at the foot of the bed and slid her feet into the warm fuzzy panda bear slippers that Jim had insisted Gloria loan her.

Outside her room the upstairs was dark. There was a night-light in the bathroom at the end of the hall, but Coralie went in the other direction and felt her way down the stairs. Halfway down she saw the glow of light from the kitchen. Someone was still up.

At the bottom of the stairs she turned and went into the room. It was empty. She looked at her watch and saw that it was only ten-thirty. She hadn't been asleep as long as she'd thought, but there didn't seem to be any other light on in the house.

Then she heard the squeaky screen door to the porch open and close, and the stamping of feet. Who would be outside in this weather, and why?

While she stood there the door opened and Jim walked in, all bundled up in his heavy jacket with a long wool scarf around his neck and a knit cap pulled down over his ears and forehead. In his gloved hand he carried a battery-powered lantern.

"Coralie." His tone bespoke his surprise. "What's the matter? I thought you were asleep."

He set the lantern on the floor, then took off his gloves, pulled off his cap and muffler and shoved them in his pockets.

"I was," she said, "but something hitting against the house woke me up. What were you doing outside in this storm?"

He unbuttoned his jacket, then removed it and hung it on the hook by the door. "I heard the noise, too, and went out to investigate. It was a TV antenna that was apparently ripped off someone's roof by the wind and carried along until it slammed into our house. It doesn't seem to have done any serious damage. At least none that I can find. I anchored it down so it won't go any farther."

It was chilly in the house even with her flannel nightie and heavy robe on, and Coralie hugged herself and shuddered. "Isn't this blizzard ever going to end?" she asked plaintively. "I've never been in such a bad storm before. It's like being trapped in a cold frozen hell."

Jim reached for her and cuddled her in the shelter of his arms. "Aw, don't be afraid, darlin'," he murmured huskily into her hair. "It won't last much longer, and it's not all that uncommon here in Idaho, although this one's come along a little later in the winter than usual."

She snuggled against his broad chest and felt warm and safe. Even after being out in below-zero weather he radiated heat, and she knew without him telling her that he'd protect her from the forces of nature or anything else that might threaten her.

How could that ex-wife of his walk away from him even if she didn't care for life on a farm? Coralie strongly suspected that if she stayed here much longer, and he asked her to, she'd follow him anywhere.

He gave her a quick hug, then relaxed his hold and stepped back. "Just let me take off my boots, and then we'll go in the living room. I was letting the fire die down before turning in, but I'll stoke it up again and we can sit in front of it and keep warm. Is that okay?"

Okay? It sounded like heaven. Even the storm couldn't scare her when she was with him. "I'd like that," she admitted, "but didn't you want to go to bed?"

She caught the double entendre after it was too late, and she felt the blush of embarrassment as his brown eyes gleamed and an amused grin twitched the corners of his mouth.

"Honey," he said wickedly, "that's an invitation no man could refuse. I think you'd better rephrase the question."

The blush grew hotter, but she was determined not to react like the innocent maiden he insisted she must be. Instead, she deliberately let her gaze roam slowly from the top of his head to his feet and back again. "Well, of course, if you don't think you're man enough for me..." she drawled.

For just a moment he looked confused, then he laughed, a hearty booming laugh, and lunged for her. A muted yelp tore from her throat as his hands caught her at the waist and lifted her off the floor to his eye level.

"I'll give you a sample and let you decide for yourself," he said, then covered her mouth with his own.

Startled, she threw her arms around his neck to balance herself, and then she was lost. Her feet were several inches off the floor as his arms closed around her waist, and he held her against him as his lips clung to hers. She'd never been kissed like this before. He was gentle but insistent, needy but controlled.

She sighed and opened to him, but he didn't ravish the inside of her mouth. Instead, he explored it lingeringly with his tongue, then nibbled tenderly on her lower lip. She nibbled back, and he groaned as his arms tightened around her.

She could have continued on forever, but he was the one who reluctantly broke it off and lowered her slowly down his body to the floor. She was left in no doubt as to how powerfully their kiss had affected him, and she couldn't understand why he stopped. She certainly hadn't been resisting.

He must have seen her confusion in her eyes, because he cupped her chin with his hand and lifted her face so he could look at her. "I knew the minute I saw you that you were going to be a serious threat to my peace of mind and well-being."

His tone was gravelly, but his lips were gentle as they caressed her closed eyelids, first one, then the other, sending prickles of pleasure down her spine. "You've just proven me right. It's been a long time since I've had a woman, and I don't trust my self-control, so we'd better cool it."

She knew he was right. Her peace of mind and self-control were already shattered, but even so her disappointment was painful. "Do you want me to go back upstairs to my room?"

His glance searched her face before he shook his head. "No, I want you to sit with me down here for a while, but no more kissing, okay?"

She felt her lips tremble, but made an effort to keep her voice steady. "Okay. You take off your boots and I'll go stir up the fire in the fireplace."

He chuckled. "Stirring up fires in things is what you do best, darlin'. Take it from one who knows."

She loved it when he said things like that, then chided herself for her inconsistency. They'd both agreed that Buck's hopes for a mail order marriage between them was out of the question. They were strangers, they had nothing in common, she was too young for his taste and she had no desire to be a mother to his two spoiled daughters.

So why did her heart speed up every time he came nearer? Why did she quiver when he touched her? And why didn't she run upstairs and lock herself in her room instead of flirting with heartbreak by staying down here with him and hoping he'd forget why he shouldn't kiss her and do it again, and again, and again....

She shivered with desire, but he mistook it for a chill. "Run along now and get that fire going before you catch cold," he said as he hunkered down to unlace his boots.

She went to the living room and stirred up the embers, then added another log. The fireplace was truly beautiful. Jim had told her it was constructed by his grandfather from native rock chipped out of the craggy mountain peaks nearby when he'd built the house for his new bride, Jim's grandmother.

The room was large and paneled in knotty pine. Not the synthetic sheets like the ones used today, but the real thing. There were also heavily lined drapes at the windows and thick carpet on the floor. When he'd shown her through the house earlier in the day Jim had assured her that it was usually fairly easy to heat even in the coldest weather, but the gale force winds they were having now, combined with the arctic temperatures, blew the cold air in despite the tightness of the building.

As she knelt there, fanning the flame to catch the wood, she heard Jim padding around the kitchen and wondered what he was doing. The rattle of cupboard doors and pans brought her to her feet.

"What are you doing out there?" she called as she hurried through the dining room.

"I'm fixing us some hot chocolate," he said as she came through the door and saw him standing at the stove.

"You do like it, don't you?" he asked and stirred the contents of the pan on the burner with a long-handled spoon. "My kids love it, and it'll warm you up in a hurry."

"Sure I do," she assured him as the sweet aroma of chocolate tweaked her nostrils, "but I haven't had any in years."

She noticed he'd taken off his boots and was walking around in the heavy woolen socks he wore inside them.

"In that case you've got a treat coming," he said cheerfully and poured the contents of the pan into two thick mugs that had been set out on the counter.

He picked up one of them and handed it to her. "Here, take a sip, but be careful not to burn your mouth." He put the pan in the sink and ran water into it. "Do you want marshmallows?"

"No, no thank you," she said hastily. "There's too many calories in this as it is without adding marshmallows."

His gaze roamed over her. "Surely you're not trying to lose weight," he said seriously. "You look just right to me."

She smiled, pleased with his compliment. "No, but I don't want to gain any, either. I tend to do that rather easily and then it's difficult to lose."

He turned off the kitchen light and they went into the living room where the fire in the fireplace was now burning brightly. Jim walked over to the couch and put his cup on the coffee table. "Sit down," he told her. "I'll be right back."

He took off and was back in a minute with a large maroon blanket. Sitting down at the end of the couch, he patted the seat next to him. "Slide over here beside me," he instructed and unfolded the cover.

She put her cup on the table also and moved down so that their hips and thighs were touching. He spread the blanket over their laps, then shut off the lamp on the end table and shifted his body so that he was partially turned toward her and could put his arms around her.

"There," he said as he tucked the cover around them. "This should keep you warm. Are you comfortable?"

Comfortable? She snuggled against him and buried herself in his embrace. The house was dark now except for the blazing fire that cast dancing shadows about the room. She'd never felt so contented before in her life. "Oh, yes," she breathed. "Are you?"

"You better believe it," he murmured into her hair. "You know, I guess this is what they used to call 'bundling' back in the last century before they had central heat. My grandma told me about it once when I was just a little kid. She said when it was too cold for young couples to sit in the chilly room in the evenings and court they'd wrap up together in a blanket."

Coralie raised her head to look at him and see if he was kidding, but he seemed serious. "My goodness, that seems pretty cozy for those Victorian days."

"It's pretty cozy for these enlightened days, too," he muttered and rubbed his cheek in her hair. "I remember Grandma saying there were quite a few shotgun weddings and early babies around that time." He chuckled. "I don't know whether she ever caught on to the cause and effect or not."

Coralie laughed. "Don't sell your granny short. I'll bet she wasn't nearly as naive as you like to think. She probably bundled a few times with her young man, too."

Jim feigned a look of shock. "My granny! Surely you jest."

"So how long were she and your grandfather married before their first baby came along?" Coralie asked impishly.

Jim seemed to consider. "Would you believe seven months? But of course the child was premature," he hastened to assure her. "He only weighed eight pounds."

She sputtered with laughter and punched him on the arm with her fist. "You nut," she exclaimed. "Shame on you telling tales on your poor old grandmother."

"Poor old grandmother my eye," he said. "That lady was an early-day women's libber. She marched in support of Margaret Sanger for the right to dispense birth control information, and she fought tirelessly for women's right to vote. Oh, and by the way, I was just kidding about the baby.

She and Grandpa were married five years before my Uncle Harry was born, and ten years before Buck came along."

Without taking his arm from around her he reached out with the other one and picked up her cup. "Here," he said and handed it to her. "Better drink this before it gets cold."

He reached again and picked up his own. He took a swallow and so did she. "Tastes good," he said, "even if I did make it myself."

"It's delicious," she agreed, and they both drank some more, then put their cups on the low coffee table.

He settled back and pulled the blanket up around her shoulders. "Are you warm enough now?"

Warm enough? She'd never felt so blissfully content before in her whole life. His chest was such a snug pillow. She could feel his strong steady heartbeat underneath the soft black-and-red plaid flannel shirt he wore.

"Oh, yes," she answered. "You generate so much heat that curling up with you is like snuggling up to a furry bear.

He chuckled. "That's partly your fault. You've raised my temperature by several degrees. Do you realize this is the first time we've been alone together since you got here?"

"Yes. I only catch glimpses of you as you come and go. I've seen a lot more of Buck. He's such a nice man."

"I think he's pretty special, too," Jim agreed, and she heard the affection in his tone. "I don't know what I'd have done without him since Marsha left. He's always there with either help or advice, whichever is needed. The only time he messed up was when he registered me in that lonely-hearts club without my knowledge. Other than that he's been a strong, steadying influence on all of us."

Coralie felt the sharp sting of rejection at his words and lifted her head as she straightened up. "I've already apologized for being such a bother," she said. "I don't know what more I can say. I'll leave just as soon as the storm is over and the roads are open again, but until then I'm afraid you're stuck with me."

He blinked and shook his head, his expression one of surprise and dismay. "Good Lord, Coralie, don't be so thin-skinned. I wasn't talking about you, although I can understand why you might think I was. I'm talking about Buck's interference when I'd told him emphatically that I wasn't interested in getting married again, and certainly not to someone I'd met through a want ad!"

His hands cupped her shoulders now as though he'd like to shake her. "It caused a lot of trouble and inconvenience for you, too, so why do you feel I'm criticizing you every time I mention it? I should think you'd be as upset with him as I am."

"I take it personally," she said, "because it embarrasses me so to think that I actually answered an ad like that. I don't know what got into me. I can't even blame Kirsten for encouraging me. I'm a grown woman. I make my own decisions and my own mistakes, and I really acted like a dolt this time."

One of his hands moved from her shoulder to stroke a long strand of hair off her face, and it occurred to her that it must be pretty disheveled since she hadn't even brushed it when she got out of bed.

"Don't be so hard on yourself, honey," he said in that quiet, cajoling tone that turned her spine to jelly. "We all make mistakes. God knows, I've made more than my share. The best we can do is try not to repeat them."

"Is that why you don't want to get married again?" she asked before she even knew she was thinking it.

He looked startled, and she was afraid he was going to tell her it was none of her business, but when he spoke his voice was calm, even reflective. "Yes, it is," he admitted. "Marsha and I were only twenty when we rushed into marriage. We hadn't even had a chance to grow up yet. It was a mistake from the get go, but by the time we realized it we had one baby and another on the way. It was easier to stay married than to hassle with a divorce and child custody."

Coralie had another impertinent question and decided to gamble on his continuing good nature by asking it. "Did you love her?"

She saw the annoyance in his expression and was afraid she'd pushed him too far, but when he answered his tone was matter-of-fact. "We thought we were in love in the beginning, and later, when we were mature enough to understand the difference between lust and love, she was my wife and the mother of my children. We owed it to the kids to respect each other and raise them in a family setting. No, we weren't passionately in love, but we got along pretty well."

He guided her head back to lie on his shoulder and they both relaxed again. "Marsha didn't run away from me or from the children. She ran away from life on the farm. She hated it. The long hours of hard work, the isolation and loneliness, the ever-present specter of losing everything in a drought, or a crop failure, or swarms of locusts. Because I'd never known any way of life but farming and all the hardships that went with it, I didn't comprehend how deep her aversion to it went."

Coralie heard the anguish in his voice. "She needed my understanding, and I let her down. I can't take the chance of that ever happening again with another woman.

"This farmer is never going to take another wife."

Chapter Six

Coralie could think of no reason to believe Jim would change his mind anytime in the near future. His regret for failing to understand the depth of his wife's unhappiness was strong, but so was his determination not to repeat that failure.

Actually, he had a point. He really didn't need a wife. He and his dad were capable, self-sufficient men. They could cook, clean and do all the other things that needed done around the house. A housekeeper would be a big help because of the volume of work involved in trying to farm and keep house, too, but he'd no doubt find another one soon.

His two daughters really needed a mother, but every baby is born to just one mother. If that one is lost or gone for whatever reason, providing a substitute is a whole lot trickier than finding a housekeeper. Jim was an excellent father. He gave them love and security in abundance. It was obvious that his girls didn't want a stepmother, so he was no doubt right not to force one on them.

But what about his needs?

She rubbed her palm over his chest. "I think you're assuming too big a share of the guilt for the breakup of your marriage. Marsha could have handled it better, too. Just running away seldom solves anything."

"It solved Marsha's problem," he said, and for the first time she heard a twinge of bitterness. "She's got everything she always wanted now."

"She doesn't have her children," Coralie reminded him gently.

"Only because she didn't want them. I insisted on physical custody, but I was always willing for her to have visitation rights. She could have had the kids occasionally on weekends and school holidays, but she didn't want them. She hasn't even seen them, or talked to them...."

His voice broke, and his arms tightened around her as she nuzzled the side of his neck.

"Buck told me," she murmured, "and I don't understand how she could be like that, but it's not fair for you to condemn all women for the faults of just one. Do you really want to spend the rest of your life alone? Gloria and Amber are growing up fast. They won't be living at home for many more years."

"I'll worry about that when the time comes," he said into her hair. "Until then I'm a confirmed bachelor."

"But don't you miss having a...a..."

She stumbled over the term, but Jim said it for her. "A bed partner? Damn right I do. I didn't say I never get lonely." He chuckled. "Or restless. But take it from me, lust is not a good basis for a marriage. It doesn't last, and when it's cooled off there's nothing left to bind a man and a woman together except obligation, and that can be a trap."

It sounded to her as if that trap had closed on his heart and taken it prisoner. What a shame, because he had so much to give a woman if he truly loved her. She hadn't known him long, but she was sure of that.

"I think we've talked enough about me," he said, changing the subject. "Tell me about you. Why did you answer that ad for a mail order bride? You're not going to convince me that you don't know plenty of men who want to take you out."

"If by 'take me out' you mean take me to bed, then you're right, but that's all they want," she answered frankly. "Most men around my age don't want to get married, they just want a good time. I'm not desperate enough to play their games. I would like to have a husband and a family, but I don't believe that playing musical beds is the way to attract the type of man I want."

He raised his head and looked down at her. "And answering ads in a lonely-hearts magazine is?" he asked dubiously.

His perfectly natural question made her feel like a floozy, and again she fought that unwelcome blush. "No, of course not. I told you, my roommate egged me on, but it was your letters—I mean, Buck's letters purporting to be you—that caught my interest. They were so sweet and homey with an undertone of loneliness... I'm sorry I didn't bring them with me so you could read them. I assume that you've read the ones I wrote to him?"

Jim gathered her close again and laid his cheek on the top of her head. "Yes, I insisted on reading them, and they were also sweet and homey with just an undertone of loneliness. You and Buck seem to have a lot in common. Maybe you should marry him."

She heard the smile in his voice, but she wasn't amused. Father and son were a lot alike, and she suspected that if Jim had written those letters they would have had the same tone.

"Maybe I would if he'd ask me," she said testily. "He'd be a good husband. How long ago did you lose your mother?"

"She died shortly after Amber was born," Jim said thoughtfully. "That's when things began to go really wrong with Marsha and me. With Mom gone all the work of a farm wife fell to Marsha, as well as taking care of two babies who needed almost constant attention. I hired the wife of one of the farmhands to help, but even so it was a big job and a lot of responsibility."

It sounded like plain old drudgery to Coralie, and she understood a little better why Marsha finally broke under it. "Had she ever lived on a farm before she married you?"

"Oh, sure. She was born and raised on one, and she always hated it. Her dad was a farmer same as mine, and her lifelong ambition had been to get out of the country and live in the city. Any city."

"But she knew you were a farmer, so why did she marry you?"

Jim sighed. "Because we were the victims of the well-known conflict between raging hormones and old-fashioned morals. We'd both been taught that it was wrong to set up housekeeping together until after you were married, and we were in a hurry. Gloria was born ten months later, and Amber barely two years after that. Then Mom died and there was no escape. Dad needed us here, and I wasn't going to let him either work himself to death or lose the farm. Marsha never forgave me."

Coralie heard the guilt and remorse in his voice. He blamed himself for the breakup of his marriage, but it seemed to her that Marsha hadn't tried very hard to keep it together, either.

She let her hands roam over his chest again. "I'm sorry you were both so unhappy, but you shouldn't shoulder all the blame. It takes two to break up a marriage, and she didn't have to leave the way she did and abandon her children."

She felt his heart speed up, and he moved one hand to cup her breast. Even through her robe and nightie his touch sent a wave of pleasure rolling through her.

"I don't want to talk about my ex-wife anymore," he murmured against her ear. "I can't focus on her when I've got you in my arms."

He nibbled on her lobe and the wave of pleasure became a tide. She wanted to please him, too, and her fingers tackled the buttons of his shirt. They opened easily, and when she slipped her hand inside she was surprised to find that he wasn't wearing an undershirt in this cold climate. Her palm touched his bare flesh.

He gasped and his hand tightened on her breast, then released it to pull down the zipper on her robe and cup it through the thinner covering of her flannel nightie. "How many layers of clothing are you wearing?" he asked huskily.

Her own voice was shaky when she answered. "That's the last. There are buttons at the throat, but they don't open very far...."

He ran his thumb lightly back and forth over her nipple, making her squirm with excitement. "It's just as well," he said and trailed kisses across her cheek. "This is all the temptation I can handle."

He leaned down and kissed the sensitized nipple, and she put her arms around his neck and rubbed her cheek in his hair. For a big man he was amazingly gentle. His hands skimmed over her lightly and yet they trailed fire in their wake. His lips were rough from the cold and exposure, but there was only tenderness in their caresses on her bare skin. She could imagine what it would be like to have him take her nipple in his mouth.

The very thought of it made her shiver and silently curse the intrusive flannel.

"Coralie, this is madness," he moaned and raised his head slightly to explore the sensitive hollow of her throat with his tongue.

"I know," she agreed raggedly as she stroked her fingers through his thick black hair.

"I love your hair," she murmured and stroked it again. "It's so... so vibrant. I can feel the electricity in it."

"It's not only my hair that's charged," he muttered seductively. "My whole body vibrates when you touch me. A little more of this and I'm not going to be able to stop."

"Me, either," she whispered, too befuddled in mind and libido to care about the consequences if that happened.

His hand that had been teasing her breast slid downward to her hip, leaving a path of heat in its wake. Expectantly, she shifted toward him as he turned to her until their bodies were pressed together. With a short insistent movement he put his hand on her derriere and pushed her against the hardness of his groin.

Coralie whimpered as a surge of desire left her breathless with need, and her arms tightened around his neck. His spanned her waist and held her to him. She raised her face and he lowered his head to capture her lips in a forbidden kiss.

For a fleeting moment she remembered why they'd both agreed kissing was a no-no, a caress too hot to handle, but the thought was lost in the ecstasy that ebbed and flowed through her whole being as his mouth masterfully made love to hers.

She responded in ways she hadn't even known about as she followed his lead. If this was a prelude to his performance in bed, then his wife must have been an unfeeling iceberg if it didn't more than make up to her for having to live on the farm!

A loud pop from the fireplace snapped them out of their erotic delirium as they broke off the kiss and looked toward the noise. The fire had burned down to embers again and left only a glow.

"If you believe in guardian angels I think ours is trying to tell us something," Jim said shakily. "It's definitely time to retire to our separate rooms. Will you be all right alone? Are you still afraid of the storm?"

Coralie wondered if it would be a sin to tell a guardian angel to mind her own business. "No, I'll be fine," she assured him unenthusiastically.

He hugged her to him. "Do I owe you an apology?" he murmured.

She shook her head beneath his chin. "No. Not at all." Her voice was almost a whisper. "It was the most enjoyable kiss I ever had."

And that was a classic understatement.

"Me, too," he said, but she figured he was just saying that to make her feel good. After all, he was a lot older, more experienced and he'd been married.

"It's not going to happen again, though," he continued. "I promise to keep better control of myself. You won't need to worry that I'll be hitting on you all the time you're here."

She wished he wouldn't promise that, although she knew he was only thinking of her best interest. "You weren't hitting on me," she protested. "In case you didn't notice, I wasn't resisting."

He kissed the top of her head. "Oh, I noticed, believe me I did, and I enjoyed every second of it. But that still doesn't make it right."

He threw back the blanket they'd been wrapped in and stood, then reached out his hand to help her up. "Come on, I'll walk upstairs with you, then come back and lock up the house."

She didn't need to be escorted to her room, but she wasn't going to refuse his company. She put her hand in his, again forgetting that it was the burned one, and when he pulled her up she couldn't stifle a cry of pain.

"Oh, sweetheart, I'm sorry," he said and quickly loosened his hold, but didn't release her. Instead, he raised the throbbing palm to his mouth and tenderly kissed the redness on each finger, then the larger burn below.

"Such exquisite little hands," he murmured sadly. "They sure as hell weren't meant for farm work. Do you want some ice?"

No man had ever kissed her hand before, and she was surprised by the strong sensations it aroused in her. "No, thanks, it's okay," she replied. "It only hurts when I forget and try to use it."

He kissed it again, then released it, put his arm around her waist and headed for the stairs.

At her doorway he reached inside and switched on the light, then turned to her. She didn't know what to expect, but if he should sweep her off her feet and carry her to the bed with every intention of having his way with her she knew she wouldn't resist. She was ashamed of herself for being so...so available...with him, but she couldn't help it. He played her heartstrings like a harp!

He didn't carry her off to bed, but cupped her head with his two hands and tipped her face upward. His deep brown eyes were clouded with desire and his voice was husky as he murmured, "Good night, sweetheart, and thank you for lighting up my life even if only for a few days."

He kissed her quickly on the tip of her nose, then turned and walked away.

The storm blew itself out sometime during the night, and Coralie woke to blessed stillness and bright sunshine. Eagerly, she reached for her robe, slid her feet into her slippers and hurried to the window.

The view from her second-story room was magnificent. Five or six feet of white unsullied snow, blinding in the rays of the sun, covered everything, including the ridge of hills in the background. It banked high against the outbuildings, blanketed the roofs and bowed the smaller tree branches under its weight. A big old willow wept drooping tears of ice, and anything smaller was hidden under the frozen majesty.

This was her first glimpse of the farm, and if it was always this beautiful she could understand why Jim loved it so. Focusing her gaze closer to the house she noticed him pushing a snowblower from the back door to the barn.

Quickly, she dressed in jeans, a heavy sweatshirt and her midcalf-length boots, then grabbed her coat and ran down the stairs. She was pulling the coat on when she got to the kitchen where Buck was loading the dishwasher.

"Whoa, girl," he said. "Where you goin' in such a hurry?"

"Hi, Buck," she called cheerfully as she hurried past him. "I'm going out to help Jim shovel snow."

"Now hold on there." His commanding tone brought her to a halt. "You can't go outside in that thin coat, the temperature is below zero. Have some breakfast first. You'll need the extra energy if you're gonna wrestle with that snow."

The heavenly smell of fresh-perked coffee that permeated the room was tempting but... "Later. I'll have some later."

She managed a couple of more steps before he stopped her again. "You'll have it now," he said and walked over to the stove to light the burner under the skillet. "It won't take but a few minutes, that will give me time to find you something heavier to wear. There's plenty of snow to go around. We won't run out of it for weeks."

"But, Buck, I'm really not hungry—"

He picked up the percolator from a burner at the back of the stove. "Sit down and have a cup of coffee while I fix your bacon and eggs. Let's see, you like 'em over medium, don't you?"

She decided it was quicker to give in than to argue with him. "Okay," she said with a sigh, "and, yes, I do like my eggs over medium, but just one please."

She removed her coat while Buck put bacon in the frying pan. It immediately started to crackle as she backtracked to the table where she sat down. Buck poured coffee into a mug and set it in front of her. "Did you sleep well last night?" he asked.

Last night! In the excitement of waking to sunshine and no wind or snow she'd forgotten about what took place last night.

"Uh, yes. Yes, I slept very well," she stammered.

He went back to the stove and cracked an egg on the rim of the skillet, then separated the shell and let the contents fall into the pan. "I thought I heard you and Jim talkin' after I'd gone to bed," he said.

She almost choked on her coffee and knew that her face was flaming again. She'd never blushed so much in all her life as she had since she'd been here.

"Well . . . yes, you probably did," she admitted. "I woke up and the wind was blowing so hard that I was, um, uneasy, so I came downstairs. Jim was still up and we...we had some hot chocolate."

Buck turned the egg. "Jim's a nice guy to have around when you're scared, isn't he?"

Coralie nodded. She wasn't sure whether he was just making conversation or if he'd seen the two of them on the sofa. "Yes, he is. I don't think he's afraid of anything."

"He's afraid of marriage," Buck said sadly. "You like him, don't you?"

"Of course I like him. He's kind, and generous, and loving. What's not to like?"

Buck's expressive face screwed up in a frown. "Then why don't you stay around for a while. Give him a chance to discover that he's happier with you than he'll ever be without you? You must want a husband or you wouldn't have answered that ad I put in the magazine."

Coralie blushed again, but this time it was more from anger than embarrassment. "Buck, you're meddling again. Jim's love life is none of your business. Why don't you leave him alone. What do you want from him, for God's sake?"

She wished she could bite back her unkind words even before Buck's expression changed from concern to shame. "Aw, honey, I don't mean to butt in. I just want him to be happy. He needs a sweet little wife like you, and a few more babies would be nice."

She couldn't stay mad at Buck. He meant well, even though he did get out of line sometimes. Besides, the thought of feeding Jim's baby at her breast made her feel warmly maternal.

"I'm afraid that's for neither you nor me to say," she told him as gently as possible. "He's old enough to know what he wants out of life, and he's adamant about not wanting another wife. Besides, Gloria and Amber don't like me, and I'm not all that fond of them, either. I'd be a lousy stepmother."

He turned off the burner, then put the bacon and egg on a plate and brought it to her. "Naw, you wouldn't, either. You'd be good for them. You'd teach 'em how to behave properly."

Coralie couldn't help but laugh at that unlikely happening. "They'd never take orders from me, or even suggestions. Especially Gloria. No, Buck, please don't interfere. Jim has made it very clear that he's not interested in taking another wife, and you really do have to respect his wishes."

Buck poured himself a mug of coffee and sat down beside her. "Would you marry him if he asked you?" he blurted.

She was astonished at his audacity. Actually, it was an innocent audacity, even though that was something of a contradiction of terms. He simply wanted his son to be happy and saw no reason why he shouldn't help Jim to see as clearly as Buck insisted he did where that happiness lay.

"Buck, you're incorrigible," she scolded, but there was more amusement than outrage in her tone.

He looked puzzled. "*Incorrigible* isn't a word we use a lot on the farm," he said. "Is it good or bad?"

She couldn't tell whether he was teasing her or not, but she suspected he was twisting her around his little finger and knew exactly how to go about it.

She laughed. "It means I'm not going to tell you how I feel about your stubborn hunk of a son," she said as she finished her last bite of breakfast and stood. "Instead, I'm going out and help him shovel snow, and you can make whatever you want of that."

Buck beamed. "It's got to be love," he said. "No woman in her right mind would shovel snow for a man when she didn't have to if she wasn't crazy about him."

Coralie made a good-natured face at him. "You said something about finding me a heavier coat?"

It was cold outside! And so bright that it hurt her eyes as she pulled on her gloves and walked down the path Jim had blown through the snow to the barn. It was icy, and a couple of times she almost slipped and fell as she tugged her knit hat over her hair. She was thankful to Buck for loaning her his heavily quilted jacket.

Inside the barn it took her a moment to accustom her eyes to the darker interior. When she did she saw Jim as he came from one of the stalls.

He saw her at the same time and set down the pail he was carrying. "Coralie! What are you doing here?"

They kept walking toward each other. "I came to help you shovel snow," she told him.

She walked straight into his outstretched arms and he hugged her to him. "Oh, you did, did you? And how do you expect to do that with a burned hand and two-inch-long fingernails?"

She hugged him back. "They're not two inches long, but if it will make you feel better I'll cut them. Now where's my shovel?"

He rubbed his cheek against hers, and his was chilly, although his embrace was toasty. "Have you ever shoveled snow before?"

She snuggled closer, knowing she had a good excuse. It really was cold this morning. "Well, no, but I can learn. I'm a quick study."

He chuckled. "I don't doubt it, but you don't have the muscles for such heavy work. All you'd do is distract me."

She leaned her head back slightly to look at him. "Do I distract you?" The thought excited her.

"You know damn well you do," he grumbled. "Just like you're doing now. If you hadn't come out here I'd have had a path cleared halfway to the garage by now instead of standing here wondering if I can talk you into a nice long leisurely roll in the hay."

"Sounds like fun," she teased. "Your haystack or mine?"

"Coralie, dammit," he groaned. "What am I going to do with you?"

"Put me to work," she suggested. "That'll keep me too busy to distract you."

He brushed his lips across hers and back. "Yeah, but I gotta tell you, I prefer the roll in the hay," he whispered against her mouth.

"Hey, Jimmy," Buck's voice called from the open end of the building, startling Jim and Coralie into springing apart. "Need some help?"

Jim uttered a frustrated oath, but his whimsical nature couldn't resist playing into the double entendre. "No, Dad, it's been a while, but I think I can remember how," he called back as Coralie chortled with glee.

The morning flew by, and even Gloria and Amber pitched in and helped for a while. By noon when Buck called them all in for dinner Coralie was one aching lump of muscles. She hadn't realized that shoveling snow could be such hard and heavy work. Not only that but both of her hands felt as if they were rubbed raw, and although she hadn't taken off her gloves to look she was almost sure her burned hand was bleeding.

She hobbled over to the back porch and sat down on the top step. It had been cleared of snow early that morning, and the sun had pretty well dried it.

She wondered if she'd be able to stand and walk again, but sincerely doubted it. A glance around the barnyard told her she had a lot to show for her pain. They'd dug paths to all the outbuildings, and toppled the snow from the doors so they could open them. If the sun stayed out for a few days it should melt a good share of what remained in the barnyard.

She was still sitting there when Jim approached from the direction of the garage. He walked with that spring in his step as always, and she wondered how he could get around so easily when she could hardly move.

As he got closer he frowned. "Coralie, what's the matter?" He leaned over her and put his hand on her shoulder.

She managed a small smile. "Nothing that about twelve hours in a tub of hot steaming water and a month in traction won't cure," she assured him.

"Aw, honey, I'm sorry," he said regretfully. "I was so busy that I forgot you were a novice at this type of thing. Here, I'll carry you inside—"

"No," she said emphatically as he reached down to pick her up. "I don't need to be carried around like a child. I can walk."

Brave words, but she wasn't sure she could follow them up with the action. "Just help me to stand."

He put his hands under her arms and raised her gently to her feet, which also hurt from being confined in boots that hadn't yet been broken in. She clamped her teeth together to keep from moaning as he put his arm around her and assisted her to walk into the house.

Inside, he helped her out of her coat and hat, then started to pull off her gloves, but stopped abruptly when she cried out in pain. "What the..." he muttered and proceeded to peel the left one off carefully. Her palm was red and blistered.

"Damn it, Coralie," he said tightly, and gently removed the right one. As she'd feared that one was bleeding.

He swore lustily, and this time he didn't bother to ask, but swung her up into his arms and walked out of the kitchen and down the hall toward the bathroom.

"Where are you taking me?" she asked.

"I'm going to run hot water in the tub and put you in to soak," he informed her.

"You . . . you can't do that," she protested as visions of him stripping off her clothes and lowering her nude into the tub flashed through her mind.

"The hell I can't," he thundered. "Amber, come here. Now," he shouted up the stairway as they strode past it.

He carried her into the bathroom and sat her down on the closed commode lid, then hunkered down in front of her and started tugging at her boots. It hurt when he slid them off, but immediately felt better once her feet were free.

Amber came hurrying in while Jim was carefully rolling Coralie's socks off her blistered feet. "What do you want, Dad?" she asked, then caught a glimpse of Coralie's feet and hands and gasped. "What happened?"

"I'm afraid we've got a tenderfoot in our midst," he muttered, "and she's too damn stubborn to admit her limitations. I'm going to run hot water in the tub, and I want you to help her undress and climb in."

He raised his head to look at Coralie. "Do you mind if Amber helps you? I don't want you to tear open those hands and feet any more than they are already."

She knew he was right. Her muscles were so knotted up and her hands and feet so sore that she probably couldn't undress herself and get in the tub without doing more damage to them.

"No, I don't mind," she said, then looked up at Amber. "I'd appreciate it very much."

Jim's pretty blond younger daughter looked sympathetic. "Gee, I'll bet that hurts. Did you do all that just shoveling snow?" She actually sounded as if she cared whether or not Coralie was hurting.

Coralie nodded. "I'm afraid your dad's right. I am a tenderfoot." She grinned. "Or maybe I should say tender *feet*, also hands and muscles."

Amber laughed, and her delicate face glowed. "I guess you don't get to shovel much snow in California."

She looked at Jim. "You can go ahead and leave, Dad. I'll run the water."

"Thanks, sweetie." He stood. "If you need anything just holler." He winked at them both and left the room, shutting the door behind him.

Amber went to the tub and turned on the water, then adjusted it to her satisfaction and let it run. "First we better get you out of that sweatshirt," she said. "Hold up your arms."

It was painful to raise her arms, but she did, and Amber clutched the garment at the bottom and pulled it gently over Coralie's head, being extra careful not to let the heavy material of the tight cuffs brush against the wounds inside her hands.

Underneath she was wearing a white T-shirt that she'd put on as a buffer against the cold, and Amber pulled it off, too, leaving her stripped above the waist to her bra. She'd never been undressed by an adolescent before, and she couldn't help but feel embarrassed.

Amber didn't seem to share the emotion, but neither did she attempt to unfasten the bra. Instead, she said, "You'll have to stand up so I can pull your jeans down. Do you think you can? Those blisters look pretty fierce."

Coralie wasn't sure she ever wanted to move again, but she wasn't going to admit that to Jim's helpful daughter. She'd already proved to be a klutz, a troublemaker and a tenderfoot. She wasn't going to be a wimp, too.

Gritting her teeth she made a massive effort to whip her screaming muscles into action and raise herself off the commode with help from Amber, who looked fragile but had the muscle power of an athlete.

With a lot of willpower and help from Amber Coralie finally managed to shed her clothes—except for her bra and panties, which she left on in a compromise with modesty— crawl into the high old-fashioned bathtub and sink back in the steaming, bubble-scented water. She closed her eyes and groaned with relief as her tortured body began to relax, inch by throbbing inch.

"Will you be okay now?" Amber asked as she dried her hands and arms with one of the small blue towels that matched the bathroom decor.

"Yeah, I'll be fine," she answered drowsily. "Tell the others not to wait lunch on me. I'm going to soak as long as the water stays reasonably warm."

"Okay, but be careful that you don't go to sleep. If you slip down a couple of inches your nose will be underwater. I'll check on you now and then."

Coralie smiled dreamily. Amber wasn't at all like she'd pegged her. There was a sweet, sunny side to her disposition that wasn't evident when she was with Gloria.

"Thank you, Amber," she said. "It was kind of you to help me. I'm sorry I'm such a bother."

Amber put her hand on the doorknob and turned. "Oh, that's okay, you're really not so bad," she said innocently and opened the door, shutting it firmly behind her.

Chapter Seven

The following two days were also sunny, but too cold for the snow to melt. Neither was the narrow country road leading to the Buckley farm opened yet. There were too many roads and not enough equipment in the county to clear all the snow, fallen trees and other damage the blizzard had wrought.

Jim, Buck and the two girls were kept busy digging out and repairing the destruction to their own property. Coralie was surprised at how willingly Gloria and Amber worked outside, but indoors they still dropped their clothes and other possessions wherever they used them last and refused to pick up after themselves or help with the housework.

Coralie had finally had to admit her limitations. She was a liability on a farm. After the havoc she'd wreaked on herself shoveling snow Jim had refused to let her get close to a tool or a piece of machinery, so she'd volunteered to do the household duties.

For a while she'd hobbled around on her blistered feet and wore gloves on her raw hands when she used them, but by the third day after the storm ended—the fifth day of her enforced visit—she was in much better condition, and so was the digging out effort.

When they'd tuned in to the news on the radio that morning they'd learned that the last of the blocked roads would be cleared by the following day—Saturday—and the schools would reopen on Monday.

Coralie greeted the news with mixed feelings. It would be great to finally be able to get away from the farm and see the surrounding countryside. She hoped to go into Copper Canyon, explore the town and meet some of the people.

But it would also mean that there was no longer any excuse for her to stay here. When all the roads to Lewiston were opened she'd have to leave here and go... Where?

She hadn't given much thought to her future while she'd been confined to the farm with Jim and his family. She was stuck here so why sweat it?

But now she'd be free to leave. Even expected to. She knew the girls were looking forward to her departure, although she and Amber were getting along much better since Amber had assisted her the day she'd overworked shoveling snow. Gloria made no secret of her disapproval of their houseguest, though, and Coralie hadn't seen enough of Jim to know what he was thinking. He worked every day from dawn to dark, trying to get the farm back in running order. At night everyone went to bed early, exhausted from the strenuous days.

There had been no more light lovemaking between them, but the magnetism that pulled and throbbed when they were together was as strong as ever. She knew she should be happy that she could leave any day now since Jim didn't want a wife and she didn't want a free-roving lover, but the very thought of never seeing him again was agonizing.

She was going to have to make her move quickly before she got any more involved with him.

That night, when they discovered that the downed telephone lines had been fixed and they could use the phone again, she called Kirsten. Her friend and roommate was relieved and delighted to hear from her. "I've been trying every day to get through to you, but the lines were down."

"I know," Coralie said. "I've been trying to get you, too."

She told Kirsten about the severity of the storm, and about Buck's deception in signing Jim up in the lonelyhearts club without Jim's knowledge or permission.

"You mean Jim didn't even know you were coming?" Kirsten asked, her tone betraying her disbelief.

"That's right," Coralie confirmed, "and he wasn't at all happy about it. He doesn't want another wife. He had too much grief with the first one."

"You don't mean he's sending you back?" It ended as a question instead of a statement.

"Well, yes, but it was a mutual decision," Coralie lied. Much to her dismay she'd discovered in the past few days that she wasn't at all averse to the idea of having Jim Buckley for a husband. But certainly not if he was reluctant!

"I mean, we both decided that picking a marriage partner out of the want ads was pretty stupid," she continued. "I never would have come home with him from the airport the other day if all the flights out hadn't been canceled because of blizzard warnings."

"My God, is he *that* bad?" Kirsten sputtered. "Jeez, Corey, I'm sorry I talked you into—"

"No! No!" Coralie hastened to assure her. "He's not bad. He's gorgeous! A real hunk, and about the nicest man I ever met."

She knew the minute the words were out that she'd made a mistake. Now she'd have to admit that the decision not to get better acquainted was Jim's idea, not a mutual one.

"Now hold on," Kirsten said. "If he's the ideal mate, then why aren't you staying?"

Oh, damn. She really didn't want to go into all that now. "I'll explain it later," she said flatly, her tone one of dismissal. "Tell me what's going on back there."

"Nothing nearly as exciting as what you've gotten yourself into," her friend assured her.

"Have I received any mail?" Coralie asked before Kirsten could get back on the subject of Jim. "Anything from my family in South Dakota?"

"Let me see," Kirsten said, and there was a moment's pause. "You've got a couple of bills and a letter from your mother. Also a handful of advertisements."

Coralie wondered what her mother had to say. She hadn't told her parents that she was coming to Idaho in hopes of picking up a husband. She figured if it worked out she'd phone them so she could break the news gently, and if it didn't they'd never have to know about her ill-advised adventure.

"Open the letter from Mom and read it to me," she requested.

She heard Kirsten tear the envelope open, then she started to read. It was just a chatty missive with the latest news of the family back there, and as usual a plea for her to come to South Dakota and visit them as soon as possible.

Coralie thanked Kirsten, told her she didn't know yet when she'd be leaving Idaho or where she'd be going, but promised to call and let her know as soon as she'd made plans.

"You can always come back here, you know," her friend assured her. "They've already filled your job in the lab at the hospital, but they're always looking for nursing assistants."

Tears brimmed in Coralie's eyes and she realized she was homesick. She'd much prefer to go back to her job and friends in California than to strike out on her own in some strange city where she knew nobody. If it just weren't for the earthquakes!

As soon as she finished cleaning up the kitchen from supper she went upstairs to her room. Both Jim and Buck were out in the barn, and the girls were watching television in the living room. She undressed and put on her nightie, then curled up in bed with a paperback novel and tried to read.

It was a thriller by one of her favorite mystery writers, but the words kept blurring on the page as her mind refused to absorb what she was reading. Instead, it kept returning to the reality of her own problem. The mystery of *what was she going to do now?*

She'd quit her job and given up her temporary home with Kirsten in California. She could go back to both if she wanted to, but there would still be her fear of earthquakes. There didn't seem to be anywhere to get away from them in the so-called Golden State.

Idaho was pretty much earthquake free. That's one of the reasons she'd decided to answer the ad in the magazine, but she wasn't wanted here.

She could go to her parents in Winner. They had an extra bedroom and were always asking her to move back and live with them again, but they were too possessive. They wanted her to be their little girl and let them take care of her, but she was a grown woman and needed her independence.

She hadn't had much time to think about where she wanted to settle when she left California. After all, there were forty-eight states in the continental United States of America, plus Alaska and Hawaii if she wanted to leave the mainland. It shouldn't be all this hard to find a place she wanted to live.

She could find employment anywhere. There was always a need for trained health-care workers, so she didn't need to worry about getting a job.

Chicago might be nice, except that the winters were awfully cold. She didn't think she wanted to fight snow and ice for months on end if she had a choice.

Phoenix would be warm in the winter, but the desert heat could get pretty unbearable in the summertime. With a sigh she put down her book, turned off the bed light and snuggled under the covers. Her mind was just going around in circles. She'd sleep on the problem and maybe tomorrow she'd find an answer.

Late the next afternoon Jim glanced at his watch when he took it off and turned on the water faucet over the washtub in the laundry room so he could wash up for supper. It was six-thirty. Much to his relief the days were getting longer and so was his work schedule. He could keep busy outside until six now and still see what he was doing.

Today the snowplow had finally come by and opened the road into town. Also, he and Buck had cleared the private road to his dad's house, and Buck was excited about moving back there. He was an independent cuss and liked his privacy, which was fine with Jim, except he wished Buck would wait until Coralie left.

Just the thought of her leaving gave Jim a sinking feeling, and he needed all the chaperons he could get to keep him from being alone with her. He was afraid that if he got her in his arms again he'd beg her to stay, and that would be a grave error.

It was all he could do to keep himself from going to her room in the middle of the night now. If she stayed much longer he'd seduce her, and then he'd have to marry her. Not only would he not have a live-in lover with his daughters living in the house, but he knew she wouldn't agree to it, either.

The water finally started to steam. He mixed it with cold and leaned over to duck his head under the warm stream.

Reaching for the soap he lathered it and worked it into his hair, face and arms, then rinsed it off.

Not that there was anything wrong with having Coralie Dixon for a wife, he thought as he picked up the towel and dried himself off. She'd make some man a great wife, but not him. She was a city girl and knew nothing about farm life. It might be exciting to be snowed in for a few days by a blizzard, but she had no inkling of the hardships encountered in making a living on even a modern farm with all the latest equipment.

He rolled his shirtsleeves down and rebuttoned them at the cuff. No, he may be a little slow, but he was no fool, and he wasn't going to make the same mistake twice. Good sex could be a powerful incentive, but eventually the novelty would wear off and Coralie would become as discontented as Marsha had been. In time she'd leave him, too, and he wasn't going to put himself through that again.

A short while later she called them all to supper. The unmistakable smell of frying fish assailed his nostrils and made his mouth water. She'd found and defrosted the trout he and Buck had caught last summer while fishing the Snake River in Hell's Canyon.

Without being obvious about it he watched Coralie as she moved back and forth across the kitchen putting food on the table. She really was a beauty. All that golden hair that tumbled from a center part to well below her shoulders sparkled even in the dimmest light and made his fingers itch to bury themselves in it and stroke the small, well-shaped head beneath.

Her bright blue eyes seemed to probe deeply into his psyche, and her smile filled the empty spaces they found with sunshine. Tonight, she didn't smile much and it seemed to him that she looked a little sad, but her sadness just made him feel protective and needed.

She'd keep him warm all right, and their union would no doubt be pure bliss for a while. Emotionally, he could even convince himself that it would be worth having and savoring for the short time until she realized that he, his family and his farm weren't what she wanted, after all. But intellectually he knew better.

He had a gut feeling that if he ever had her and then lost her he'd never get over it.

They were about halfway through eating when Coralie mentioned that she'd talked on the phone to her friend, Kirsten, in California.

They talked about that for a few minutes, and then Coralie casually dropped her bombshell. "Oh, and Jim, I also called the airport in Lewiston."

His head jerked up even before his mind had totally assimilated her words. "The airport?" he managed to say as ice clogged his bloodstream and froze him in place.

"Yes, now that the roads are opening up again there's no need for me to stay any longer."

He felt as if he'd been jabbed in the stomach and had the wind knocked out of him. "But—"

"I didn't make a reservation because I didn't know when you'd be able to drive me back to Lewiston," she continued, "but I'd like to leave as soon as possible."

Buck broke in with a protest, and Amber said something, but Jim could only focus on the fact that Coralie was going to leave. Why did that surprise and upset him so? He'd known it was going to happen. Hell, he'd just been thinking about it, but it had always been in the future. Not now!

She spoke again, apparently in response to something Buck had said. "No, I'm not going back to California. I'm really terrified of the earthquakes that seem to be getting more frequent and more severe all the time. I've decided to go to Winner, South Dakota, and visit with my... my *relatives* there for a while."

She'd stumbled over the word *relatives,* and then Jim remembered that they'd told Gloria and Amber when he first brought her home that her parents lived in northern Idaho and she'd been visiting them when she got stuck in the airport because of the storm.

"You mean you're never going back?" Gloria asked. "What about your job?"

Jim was about to scold his daughter for her inquisitiveness when Coralie spoke first. "No, I don't plan to go back. I quit my job before I came to Idaho. I . . . I can get along without working for a couple of months or so, and I want to relocate in some other part of the country."

Good Lord. Did she quit her job before she left California because she expected to marry him and live here? Was she left stranded without a home or employment because he refused to consider a mail order wife? What would become of her now?

Without further thought he pushed back his chair and stood, then glared down at her. "Coralie, I'd like to talk to you in private." His tone was inflexible. "Please come with me."

He started around the table to help her up just as Buck jumped to his feet. "Now, Jimmy, don't—"

Jim turned and pointed a finger at his father. "And I don't want any interference from you," he said angrily, his temper only barely under control. If Buck had minded his own business in the first place none of this would ever have happened.

The older man looked crestfallen as he sank back down in his chair, and Jim knew he'd have to apologize, but not now. Silently, he took Coralie's arm and led her upstairs to his room.

Closing the door he gestured toward a chair by the desk in the part of the large bedroom that he also used as an office. He knew it was a bad idea to bring her in here with the king-size bed looming so conspicuously in its position under the wide windows, but it was the only place they could have any privacy.

She sat down, and he took the chair behind the desk. She looked frightened, and he hated that. He hadn't meant to scare her, but he had to get the answers to some very important questions.

He leaned back and tried to appear relaxed, hoping it would relax her also. "Coralie, I know you're an honest woman, and I'm counting on you to tell me the truth. Did Buck say or do anything when you two were corresponding to make you believe that you were coming here for the sole purpose of marrying me, and not just for a get-acquainted visit?"

She shook her head and opened her mouth to say something, but he spoke first. "I know you're fond of my dad and don't want to get him into any trouble, but I'm entitled to the truth. I promise I'm not going to do Buck any harm. Don't forget, I love him, too, but I can't let him off the hook until I know exactly what he did."

She let out her breath. "With God as my witness, Jim, Buck suggested I come here for exactly the reasons I told you he did. So you and I could meet and spend some time getting to know each other. At no time did I come here thinking we were going to get married."

He watched her closely, and he was almost certain she wasn't lying to him. "Then why did you quit your job and make plans to leave California permanently?"

"For the reason I told you downstairs. I don't want to live there anymore. I've been practically wiped out in three different earthquakes in three different parts of the state, and I'm terrified that the next time *I* might be the casualty instead of my possessions. That's the only reason I answered that ad in the magazine in the first place. I wanted to start over somewhere else, and that seemed like a way to do it. Obviously, I was thinking with my fear and not my good sense."

They sat in silence for a moment. Maybe it was only because he wanted so badly to believe her, but he couldn't find any reason to think she wasn't telling him the truth.

"Are you going to live with your parents in South Dakota?" he asked.

Slowly, she shook her head. "No. I love my family, but Winner isn't where I want to settle down for the rest of my life. I'll only stay there until I find a good job somewhere else. Maybe I'll try Minneapolis. I understand it's a nice city to live in."

A twinge of remembered pain reminded him of Marsha. "You don't like small-town life." It was a statement, not a question.

"I don't know," she said shakily. "I've never lived in a small town, unless Eureka qualifies. It's not exactly a city, but I liked it. That is, I did until the earthquake that shook me up for one last time."

Jim sighed. It was time to cut the ties that had been slowly binding him to her and put an end to this before there was any more emotional damage done to either of them. She was right, it was best that she leave as soon as possible.

"Well, if you're sure that's what you want, I can take you into Lewiston anytime. Why don't you call and make a reservation." He handed her the cordless phone on his desk. "If you don't remember the number just call the operator and get it."

After tossing and turning most of the night, Coralie was wakened the next morning by a knock on the door and Gloria's voice calling her name. "It's nine o'clock and dad says he should allow at least a couple of hours to drive to Lewiston since he's not sure what condition the roads are in. He says you'd better get up if you don't want to miss your flight."

Coralie's eyes snapped open and she sat straight up in bed. Good heavens, she'd not only finally fallen asleep, but she'd overslept!

"Thanks, Gloria, I'll be right down," she called back and threw off the covers.

She scrambled out of bed and pulled on the sable-colored slacks and matching pullover sweater she'd left out the night before. Her flight was due to leave at one o'clock, but they'd suggested she be at the airport an hour early in order to check in and make sure her baggage got on the same plane.

She'd intended to forgo makeup and just add a touch of lipstick, but when she looked in the bathroom mirror she was appalled at what the prospect of leaving, plus the sleepless night, had done to her usually flawless face. She looked tired and drawn, her skin pale, and bluish shadows had formed under her eyes.

She couldn't let Jim see her like this. He'd be sure that his suspicion of last night was right—that Buck had mislead her into thinking she and Jim were going to be married when she arrived here.

Quickly, she retrieved her makeup kit from the suitcase she'd packed the night before and went to work. By the time she'd finished she still looked a little woebegone, but if she could manage to smile now and then Jim probably wouldn't notice.

Back in the bedroom she stripped the bed and remade it with clean sheets. Her thoughts kept up with her hands as she worked.

She'd like to have stayed at least one more day, but once she'd convinced Jim she was leaving of her own free will he'd seemed eager to be rid of her. After practically forcing her to call the airport and make reservations he'd assured her that driving her to Lewiston today would be no trouble. He'd even stood over her while she made a call to her parents to tell them she was coming.

He'd said he wanted to make sure everything went smoothly, that she wasn't stranded anywhere along the way. She didn't doubt that he did, but it still seemed to her that he was in an awful hurry to send her off.

She smoothed the bedspread in place, then picked up her luggage and her purse and hurried downstairs. She found Jim and Buck sitting at the table in the kitchen, having coffee. Both men stood when she came in, and Jim walked over and took her suitcases.

"I'll put these in the Jeep while you sit down and have some breakfast," he told her.

She was disturbed to see that he didn't look as if he'd slept well, either. He didn't have makeup to cover the shadows under his eyes, and when he spoke his bright smile was absent. She stifled the urge to touch him and ask if he'd slept badly. He didn't want her tender, loving concern.

"Thank you, but I'm not hungry," she said instead. "We can leave anytime you want to. I'm sorry I overslept."

He walked out without replying.

"Aw, now, Coralie, don't be in such a hurry to go," Buck said, and he didn't look happy, either. "At least let me fix you something to eat first."

Her heart melted, and it was all she could do not to take him up on the invitation. He was such a sweet old man, and she hated to leave him almost as much as she hated to leave Jim.

If she wasn't careful she was going to break down and cry.

She swallowed and forced a smile. "I wish I could, Buck. Nobody cooks breakfasts as good as you do, but we're already running late, and I wouldn't want to miss my flight. I'll get something at the airport if I'm hungry."

Amber, still in her pajamas and robe, wandered in and caught sight of Coralie. The child looked disheveled, as if she'd just gotten out of bed. "Dad told us last night that you're leaving today." She sounded almost sorry.

Coralie nodded. "Yes, I am."

"How come?" Her tone was blunt and to the point.

"I've always intended to leave as soon as the roads were opened so I could get back to the airport," Coralie explained.

"Yeah, I guess," Amber said grumpily, "but why do you have to go so soon?"

Coralie blinked in astonishment. "I thought you'd be happy to see the last of me," she said. "Now you can have your bed back. I put clean sheets on it."

The girl shrugged. "I didn't mind too much sleeping in Gloria's room." She turned her attention to Buck. "Will you fix me some breakfast, Grandpa?"

"After a while," Buck answered absently. "Is Gloria up yet?"

Amber reached for a piece of cold toast from a dish on the table and took a bite. "She's awake, but she's not up. She's in bed, watching television."

Coralie bit back an unladylike oath. It's a good thing she was leaving now. Another few days and she'd start giving Jim the benefit of all her good advice on how to discipline a lazy teenager, and that would have gotten her thrown out for sure!

The sound of Jim stomping snow off his boots in the back porch saved her from saying something she shouldn't.

"It's cold out there," he warned her as he came in. "You'd better buy a heavier coat when you get to South Dakota. That one of yours is too lightweight."

"I know, and I will," she said and reached for the garment, which was hanging on the rack beside the door.

"If you're not going to eat breakfast we'd better get started," he muttered grimly. "Amber, go get Gloria so she can say goodbye to Coralie."

"Oh, no, please don't," she pleaded anxiously. "She knows I'm leaving. If she wanted to say goodbye she'd have come down. I'd really rather you didn't make a fuss over it."

Jim scowled and looked as if he were going to object, but apparently reconsidered. "All right, if that's what you want."

It wasn't at all what she wanted. She'd give anything if Gloria had come to see her off because she wanted to, but she wasn't up to any more of that young woman's scorn.

She turned to Amber. "Do you mind if I give you a hug?" she asked uncertainly.

For answer Amber nearly threw herself into Coralie's arms and hugged her back. "I'm sorry I haven't been very nice to you," she said. "I wish you wouldn't leave yet."

Coralie embraced the youngster who was no longer a child and not yet a woman. She remembered how difficult life could be when one was twelve years old, and a wave of warmth engulfed her. "I wish I didn't have to leave yet," she said softly, "but I'm way off schedule as it is. Thanks for letting me use your room."

"That's okay," Amber said shakily and stepped back.

Buck was next in line, and this time it was she who threw herself into an embrace. His. His arms tightened around her and he murmured into her ear. "Don't leave yet. Give this thing a chance. Jim would make you a good husband. Honest he would. I'd never have sent for you if I'd had any doubts on that score."

Tears burned in her eyes as she struggled to hold them back and talk without sobbing. "Jim doesn't want me," she whispered, trying for a light note, "but if you're looking for a wife I'd like to apply."

He hugged her hard, then let her go. "If I was thirty years younger I'd take you up on that," he said aloud and grinned, although his eyes were wet, too.

"Take her up on what?" Jim asked suspiciously.

"None of your business, son," Buck said, then looked at her. "Write to me, honey, so's I'll know you're all right. Promise?"

"I promise," she said and choked back a sob as she turned and opened the door.

Jim walked behind her across the porch, then took her arm when they came to the screen door and helped her down the slick cement steps. The ground underneath her feet was also slippery as he walked her around the Jeep and opened the door for her. She was still standing there, calling good-bye and waving to Buck and Amber inside the porch, when he started to retrace his steps back around the front of the car to the driver's side.

Coralie had her attention on the other two and didn't see exactly what happened, but suddenly Jim's feet went out from under him and he fell forward, smashing his head against the lower step with a terrifying crack.

She screamed and ran to him as Buck and Amber scrambled out of the porch. They all knelt beside him, and Buck turned him over before Coralie could warn him not to. Jim's eyes were rolled up in their sockets and blood streamed from his forehead.

She was aware of a lot of noise, both screaming and yelling, and for a moment she was as mindlessly terrified as the others, but then her medical training clicked in. Quickly unzipping his heavy jacket she put her head, ear down, on his chest to monitor his breathing as she felt for the pulse in his neck.

He was unconscious, and his pulse and respiration were thready. She had to get help.

Buck was kneeling beside her, making moaning noises of distress deep in his throat, and she could hear both girls calling, "Daddy," and crying. She looked at Buck and spoke loudly to get his attention. "Buck, go into the house and call 911. Tell them what's happened and to send an ambulance."

With the agility of a younger man he got to his feet and hurried up the stairs as she called after him. "Be careful! Watch for patches of ice. We don't want you to fall, too!"

While they waited for the ambulance Coralie sent the girls to bring blankets, and Buck to start his pickup truck and drive it around to where they were so they could follow the ambulance to the hospital without delay. He wanted to move Jim into the house where it was dry and warm, but she explained that moving a patient with a head injury was more dangerous than the cold.

She knew that head wounds tend to bleed profusely, but because of the possibility of a skull fracture she pressed a towel around the gash on his head instead of directly over it and applied pressure to slow down the bleeding, then tucked blankets around him in an effort to keep him as warm as possible and prevent shock. Gloria and Amber had been sent back upstairs to get dressed.

It seemed like forever that she knelt on the cold ground and kept track of Jim's vital signs, all the while talking to him softly and caressing his white face.

"Jim. This is Coralie. Can you hear me? We've called for an ambulance so just hold on. It will be here any minute." She leaned over and kissed the eyelids she'd closed earlier. "Hang in there, my darling. Don't slip any deeper into unconsciousness. Don't forget, you have a couple of daughters to finish raising, and if it means anything to you I couldn't get along without you, either."

She knew that sometimes unconscious patients could hear and feel to some degree, and there was something she wanted Jim to know even if he didn't remember it later.

She touched her cold lips to his. "I love you, sweetheart."

Chapter Eight

The ambulance arrived a few minutes later. By that time Buck had returned to the scene, and so had Gloria and Amber. They knew both paramedics, but in the hurry no one thought to introduce Coralie.

When the medic called Barney asked what had happened she stepped forward, introduced herself and explained that she was a medical assistant. She told them about Jim's fall and reported on his condition as she had observed it.

"There's no leakage of cerebrospinal fluid from the nose and ears, but he's still unconscious," she concluded.

"We'll get him to the hospital, stat," the other medic called Frank said as he reached into the back of the ambulance for a stretcher.

Carefully, they moved Jim onto it, then loaded him into the vehicle. "I want to ride with him," she said as they started to close the doors.

"Well-l-l, miss, I don't know—" Barney started to say, but Coralie cut him off.

"I'm as qualified as you," she said firmly. "I've been trained in nursing, lab work and first aid, as well as emergency procedure, and Jim is a dear friend of mine."

Frank was the younger of the two, and from the way his gaze roamed over her she could tell that he liked her long legs and high thirty-six-inch bust. "Aw, come on, Barney. She can ride back here with me."

Without waiting for an answer he took her hand and helped her into the back of the ambulance."

"The kids and I will follow you," Buck called as Frank closed the doors.

It wasn't a very long ride, but Coralie couldn't see a thing because there were no windows in the back of the vehicle. Frank was talkative and wanted to know all about her. Her mind was on monitoring Jim, and she answered Frank's questions by rote, although she did have the presence of mind to tell the same story as she and Jim had told the girls about her reason for being a guest at the Buckley farm.

They pulled up to the emergency room entrance with lights flashing and sirens blaring. The medics wheeled Jim inside where they were met by a man in a white coat, presumably a doctor. As they proceeded down the hall Coralie stayed behind in the waiting room with Buck and the girls.

"Is Daddy going to be all right?" Amber sobbed.

Coralie put her arms around the child and led her to a couch.

"I'm sure he will," she said soothingly as they sat down together. "It's not unusual for a person to lose consciousness after a blow to the head. He probably has a concussion, which will give him a king-size headache for a while, and he'll have a nasty-looking knot on his forehead, but he should wake up soon."

She wished she were as confident as she sounded. Instead, she was shaking as badly as Amber, and her mind kept reviewing all the catastrophic things that a head injury could bring on. She'd had experience with some of them in her line of work, and she was absolutely terrified for Jim.

Amber curled up in Coralie's arms and cried while Buck tried to reassure Gloria, who was sobbing on his shoulder. He didn't look as if he was doing all that great, either. His face was pasty, and the anguish he was feeling looked out of his eyes.

A few minutes later a man wearing jeans and a heavy quilted jacket came rushing through the door. He glanced around the room. "Buck," he called and hurried over to where they were sitting, "What happened? I just got the call. How's Jim?"

Buck stood and the two men hugged. "Sammy! God, but I'm glad to see you. Jimmy's hurt bad...."

His voice broke, and the man he called Sammy patted his shoulder. "We don't know that yet," he said. "Can you tell me what happened?"

"I don't really know. I didn't see... You'd better let Coralie tell you." He waved in her direction, but again forgot to introduce her.

The man turned his head to look at her. He was about Jim's age, tall with brown curly hair and green-flecked brown eyes.

Amber straightened. "Dr. Sam, will my daddy be okay?" she asked shakily.

Apparently, this was the Buckley family's doctor. He came over and sat down beside them, then reached across her and stroked Amber's disheveled hair. "I can't tell you that until I've examined him, honey, but your dad's a pretty hardheaded guy. It would take a powerful blow to damage it much. Now, do you mind if I talk to Ms...."

"I'm Coralie Dixon," she finished for him.

"Dr. Samuel Lawford," he said. "Am I to understand that you were with Jim when this happened?"

She nodded. "Yes. I've been a houseguest of the Buckleys for the past few days. Jim was getting ready to drive me to Lewiston to catch a plane when he apparently slipped on a patch of ice and fell, bumping his head on the concrete step and knocking him unconscious. That happened about..." She looked at her watch. "About an hour ago. We called 911 for an ambulance, and he was still unconscious when we got him to the hospital."

"I see," the doctor said and stood. "I'll go have a look at him and get back to you as soon as possible."

It seemed like forever before Dr. Lawford reappeared, and in the interval Coralie phoned her parents to tell them she'd missed her flight and would let them know when she'd be able to book another.

After that she kept busy supplying the others with colas, coffee and candy from the vending machine. No one was hungry, but it gave them something else to think about while they waited.

Finally, the doctor came back, and he was wearing a welcome smile. "Jim's going to be all right," he said, and they all heaved sighs of relief.

Buck was the first to speak. "Are you sure, Sam?"

The doctor nodded. "As sure as I can be until he regains consciousness. He has a concussion and a sprained ankle, but there's no skull fracture, and his vitals have stabilized."

Coralie felt dizzy with relief.

"Can we see him?" Both girls and Buck spoke in unison.

Dr. Sam shook his head. "Not yet. I've got him in recovery where he can be monitored until he regains consciousness. He should be coming out of that anytime now. He seems to hear when you talk to him, but hasn't spoken yet. Why don't you go on home. I'll call you when he can have visitors."

None of them would agree to that, but Coralie had a suggestion. "Dr. Lawford, I'm a medical assistant and I've been working with those skills for more than two years. If

you'll let me sit with Jim it would take some of the load off
the regular nursing staff."

He hesitated a moment. "Yeah. Sure, that sounds good,
if it's okay with his family." Dr. Sam looked at Buck and the
girls.

"That's fine with us," Buck said without consulting his
granddaughters. "Let her sit with him, but the rest of us
aren't leavin' the hospital until he wakes up."

He looked at Gloria and Amber, and they nodded agreement.

"It's all set, then," the doctor said as he stood. "Come
with me, Ms. Dixon, and I'll take you to your patient."

"Please, call me Coralie," she said as she followed him
out.

"And I'm Sam. Jim and I have known each other all our
lives. He's the best friend I've got." His brow wrinkled.
"But I don't remember him mentioning you."

She smiled. "We've only known each other since the day
the blizzard started. I was stranded in the airport at Lewiston so Jim brought me home with him to wait out the storm.
In fact, we were getting ready to go back there this morning
when Jim fell and hurt himself."

She glanced at her watch. "My flight just left without
me."

Sam chuckled and turned them both into a room across
the hall from the nursing station. "Can't say that I'm sorry
to hear it. Jim's going to need help for a while. I believe he's
between housekeepers again."

There were two beds in the all-white room, but only one
was occupied. Jim lay on his back in the white metal bed to
her left, and the head was raised slightly. Both she and Sam
walked over to stand on either side of it. The patient's face
was as white as the bedding, and only the amount of black
hair not covered by the bandage provided contrast.

The doctor put his hand on Jim's shoulder and shook
gingerly. "Jim. Can you hear me? Open your eyes. I've

brought someone to see you, and believe me, you're not going to want to miss her."

Jim's eyelids twitched, but didn't open. Sam tried again, this time slapping his cheek gently. "Come on, guy. Open up. You've slept long enough. Buck and the kids are worried."

The lids flickered again, but he turned his head away from the sound of Sam's voice, as if trying to get away from it.

Jim's hands were laying on his chest, and Coralie reached out and took one of them in both of hers. "Jim," she said softly. "I'm so sorry you fell and hurt yourself."

His lids fluttered, but although they didn't open he slipped his hand out of hers and reached up to touch her face.

"Coralie?" It was merely a whisper, but both she and Sam heard it.

She nearly burst with happiness. "Yes, love. Why don't you open your eyes and look at me?" she said tenderly.

He blinked a couple of times. Then, laboriously, as if they were weighted, he opened his eyes.

He looked right at her, and she felt tears gathering in her own as she took his hand and kissed the palm. "It's about time you joined the rest of us," she said and lowered his arm to hold his hand between her breasts. "We were worried."

"You . . . you didn't leave." He sounded anxious, and a pang of sorrow clutched at her. Was he disappointed?

"No, I didn't," she confirmed. "I couldn't until I knew you were going to be all right. Do you mind?"

He closed his eyes again, as if they were too heavy to keep open. "I'm glad," he whispered and relaxed.

Her gaze flew to the doctor, and he apparently read her concern. "Don't worry," he said. "He's just dozing."

He looked pointedly at her hand holding Jim's and smiled. "Why don't you stay here with him, and I'll go get Buck and the kids. They can come in and see for themselves that he's all right. But now that he's conscious you'll all have to leave. He needs rest."

Coralie caressed Jim's cheek and the side of his forehead that wasn't bandaged until she heard multiple footsteps in the hall. Then she put his hand down and stepped back to allow Buck and the girls access to him.

She retreated to a corner of the room while his family hovered anxiously around him. She was, after all, an outsider. They wouldn't want her crowding in and taking up precious space at the bedside.

Jim apparently opened his eyes again, because they all talked to him, although she didn't hear his answers.

After a few minutes Dr. Sam came in and shooed them out. "Sorry, but you'll have to leave now. As I told Amber, Jim's a hardheaded cuss, but even he needs to rest after a blow like he took. He'll be bright eyed and bushy tailed by this evening, though. You can come back and visit him after supper."

Coralie waited until Buck and the kids had said goodbye and were leaving the room before she returned to the bedside. The doctor was still standing there, too, and Jim smiled when she leaned over the bed and into his line of vision.

He reached out and took her hand. "Stay with me," he said quietly.

His request sent her heart pounding. "I'd like to, but the doctor says—"

"What does he know?" Jim grinned up at the physician. "He spends most of his time delivering babies."

Dr. Sam chuckled. "Smart ass," he said affectionately. "Just wait until you start begging me for pills to relieve the monster headache you're going to have a little later on."

"Regular little Mary Sunshine, aren't you," Jim grumbled. "Now go on, get out of here and leave us alone."

"Okay," Sam retorted, "I'll tell the others to go on without Coralie, but just remember, don't do anything I wouldn't do."

"Ha," Jim chortled, then winced with pain. "That's easy. There's not a damn thing you wouldn't do. Now shut the door when you leave and put a Do Not Disturb sign on it."

Sam laughed. "Like hell I will. You need your rest." But nevertheless he shut the door behind him.

Coralie felt a slight blush at the two men's good-natured bantering, and Jim squeezed her hand and pulled her down to sit on the side of the bed.

She gently ran a finger along his jawline. "You scared us all half to death," she murmured. "How do you feel? Does your head hurt?"

"Don't ask," he groaned. "Just lie down here with me."

Her heart jumped with joy, but her knowledge of hospital rules restrained her. "It's not allowed. The nurse will throw me out," she explained as she leaned over and brushed her lips to his temple.

"She'll have to wrestle you away from me first," he whispered, "and I'm bigger than she is."

Coralie bent over and took off her boots, then snuggled down beside him. She'd wait until they got caught before worrying about protocol.

He held her close, and within minutes he was asleep again. His breathing was deep and steady, and his heartbeat normal. When she was sure it was going to stay that way, and that he was sleeping soundly, she carefully disengaged herself from him and got up.

He slept for the next hour while she sat in a chair beside him. Then the nurse came in and woke him to check his state of consciousness and sense of orientation by asking him his name, address, telephone number and what day it was.

He answered drowsily but correctly, and when she left he looked at Coralie and muttered accusingly, "You got out of bed."

She stood and again took his hand. "Yes, but I stayed there until you were asleep. I had to get special permission from the doctor to be here, and they really would throw me out if they caught me in bed with you.''

''Then I'll go home,'' he said and fell asleep again.

Coralie devoutly hoped he'd forget that statement before he woke up. She knew Dr. Sam wanted to keep him in the hospital overnight for observation, and she had enough medical expertise to know that a head injury could be tricky as well as dangerous.

An hour later another nurse checked him again. He was more alert this time, but also in a great deal of pain so she gave him an injection that put him back to sleep.

When the third hour rolled around the nurse brought his supper tray with her. She asked Coralie if she'd like a tray, too, and she said she would, so the nurse brought her one.

Jim was still a little groggy from the medication, but it had also eased the pain in his head. He was able to tolerate having the bed cranked up to a half-sitting position while he ate.

When they finished their meal Coralie took the trays out and put them on the cart in the hall, then took a quick side trip to the nearest rest room. When she returned to the recovery room Jim was talking on the bedside telephone.

''Hi, Dad,'' he said, then waited while Buck said something. ''I'm okay, just a little groggy. Yeah, that's what I'm calling you about. I want you to come and get me.''

Coralie gasped. ''Jim, no!''

He held up his hand for silence, then spoke into the phone again. ''Oh, you know Sam. He's like a mother hen with his patients, but I can sleep at home just as well as I can here. How soon can you come?''

Coralie made a lunge for the phone. ''Jim, darn it!'' she cried as he held it against his chest and refused to give it to her. ''You can't leave unless the doctor says so.''

He glared at her. ''Of course I can. I'm as capable of signing myself out of a hospital as anyone else. Now settle down and let me talk to Buck.''

She couldn't wrestle with him without taking the chance of injuring him even more. At the very least all the jostling around would give him a humongous headache. Damn! Why did he have to be so stubborn.

Without another word she turned and marched out of the room to the nurses' station. There was an older, heavyset nurse behind the desk who looked up when she heard Coralie's boots stomping on the tile floor.

"Is Dr. Lawford in the hospital?" Coralie asked.

"We're expecting him anytime," the nurse said.

"Well, you'd better call him and tell him that Jim Buckley is making arrangements to check himself out and go home."

"You're not serious?" the nurse said as she pushed back her chair and got up.

"Go see for yourself!" Coralie advised angrily. "He thinks he's superman."

She followed the nurse into the recovery room just as Jim hung up the phone. "Thinking of leaving us, Jim?" she asked sarcastically.

"Aw, come on, Millie," he said in his best wheedling tone. "I can't lay around here just because I bumped my head. I've got a farm to run, kids to raise—"

"And a nurse of your very own?" Millie obviously knew Jim well enough to hold her own with him.

Jim grinned. "Yeah. How about that."

"You've also got a brain that's going to turn to mush if you do it any more damage," she threatened.

Jim eyed her suspiciously. "Oh? Sam said there was no contusion."

She looked startled. "There isn't, but—"

"Or hematoma?"

"Well, no, but—"

Jim pounced. "Then if there's no damage to brain tissue or blood leakage why are you threatening me with dire consequences just because I want to check out of this charming hellhole?''

"Okay, Buckley," she said. "If you're smart enough to know all that, then you're smart enough to know why you should stay here until Dr. Sam says you're ready to be discharged."

Jim grinned. "Maybe, but like you say, I've got my very own nurse at home. I can't get any more attention here than that."

"Probably not." Millie sounded more or less resigned. "But you're not going anywhere until Dr. Sam checks you out, and that's not a threat, it's a promise."

She turned and flounced out of the room.

Jim sighed and leaned back against his pillow. His face was ashen and pinched, and she knew all the fuss had skyrocketed his headache to new heights.

Sitting down on the side of the bed she stroked his cheek. "Now see what you've done," she said softly. "Why are you being so stubborn, Jim? You know you don't feel well enough to go home. The ride in the car over those bumpy roads will be agonizing."

He reached up and caressed her face with his fingertips. "Hey, I'm no stranger to pain," he said. "I went through college on a football scholarship and got toughened up real good. Had my share of injuries on farm equipment, too, and I don't like hospitals. I was just kidding with Millie. I promise not to be a bother to you. Buck could take you to the airport tomorrow if you're still intent on leaving."

She leaned down and brushed her lips across his. "Taking care of you would never be a bother to me, and I have no intention of leaving until you're fully recovered," she murmured against the side of his mouth before she sat up again. "But promise you won't be pigheaded about it if Dr. Sam insists that you stay here."

Before he could answer, Sam's voice boomed across the room. "What's this I hear about you wanting to go home?"

Startled, Coralie jumped up and turned around. The doctor strode to the other side of the bed and glared at Jim. "A head injury isn't the same as a broken collarbone or fractured ribs, both of which you're familiar with. I'm not going to release you until I'm sure there aren't going to be any repercussions."

Jim closed his eyes. "Don't get your drawers in a twist, Sam. I'm okay and you know it. I just want to sleep at home instead of here. I promise not to plow the back forty or shovel any more snow for a while."

"How can I be sure of that?" Sam asked suspiciously.

"Because I'll call you if he does," Coralie heard herself say. She knew Jim well enough to know he'd go home whether the doctor signed him out or not. She might as well save him all the upheaval that would cause.

"I agree that he should stay here," she continued, "but if he insists on leaving I'll take care of him. I'm good at what I do, and I'll report to you immediately if he gets out of line."

"Jeez," Jim muttered. "You'd think I was a kid who got hurt on the playground."

"If you're going to act like one we're going to treat you like one," Sam growled. "Let me check you over one last time, and if you're still perkin' along nicely I'll sign the release."

Buck and the girls arrived a short time later with pajamas, slippers and a heavy full-length overcoat for Jim. He was waiting for them with a large bottle of pain pills, another of antibiotics and a wheelchair to wheel him out in.

"Hospital rules, and besides, you won't be able to walk on that sprained ankle for a while," Sam informed him when he protested that he didn't need the wheelchair. "I'll drop around tomorrow and see how you're doing. Meanwhile, go to bed and stay there."

"I thought doctors didn't make house calls anymore," Jim said with a smile of gratitude for the special treatment.

"Most don't," Sam agreed gruffly. "Only those like me who can't afford to lose a best friend. Now get out of here and try not to do any more damage to yourself."

He punched Jim affectionately on the shoulder and received a friendly punch in return.

Back at the farm Buck and Coralie helped Jim hobble into the house while Gloria and Amber opened the doors and cleared the way. They took him into the downstairs bedroom that his dad used. Buck had been sleeping in his own house since they'd cleared a path to it through the snow.

Coralie turned back the covers and the girls helped Jim out of his overcoat before he dropped down on the bed with a moan. He closed his eyes and put his hands to his head, and she knew the agony he must be suffering. Thank God there was a bedroom down here so he didn't have to hop on one foot up all those stairs to his own room. That would have been even more torturous.

She sent the others away, then removed his slippers and pulled the sheet and blankets over him. "I'm sorry," she said as she turned off the bedside lamp, then leaned down and kissed him lightly on the mouth. "Dr. Sam gave you all the sedative he could to help you through the ordeal of traveling, so I can't give you more for several hours. You'll go to sleep as soon as you relax, though, and you'll feel better when you wake up."

He put his hands down and picked up one of hers. "Aren't you going to say, 'I told you so'?" He groaned.

She squeezed his hand. "I hardly think you need that."

"You're so sweet," he murmured, and within a few minutes he was asleep.

Coralie waited until she was sure he was resting peacefully, then went to join the others in the living room. They were watching television, but turned their attention to her.

"How is he?" Buck asked anxiously.

"Are you sure Daddy's going to be all right?" Gloria was anxious, too, as was Amber who's red eyes betrayed that she'd been crying.

"He's asleep now," Coralie assured them in her best professional tone. "Dr. Sam has him heavily sedated, so he'll probably sleep through the night except for a few minutes when I have to wake him every hour to check on his orientation. He won't feel very well for the next couple of days, and he'll have trouble getting around until his ankle is better, but after that he should be good as new."

They all looked greatly relieved.

"Will you..." Gloria began, then swallowed and started again, as if the words stuck in her throat. "Will you stay here until he's better?"

Was that a smidgen of hope Coralie heard in Jim's daughter's tone? That was the last thing she'd have expected, but maybe...

"I will if he wants me to," Coralie assured her. "If you all want me to...."

Buck looked pleased as he bounded out of his chair. "Of course we want you to!" he said emphatically. "We not only want you, we need you. Jim needs you. The kids and I don't know the first thing about takin' care of someone who's hurt like he is. We'd be honored if you'd stay."

"Yeah, Coralie, please stay," Amber chimed in.

Coralie intended to remain as long as she was needed, but she'd like to have Gloria's consent, too.

She looked at the teenager. "Gloria?"

Jim's other daughter hesitated a moment, then nodded. "Yes, we need your help."

It wasn't exactly an overwhelming mandate on the girl's part, but it was a positive vote that was more of a welcome than anything she'd uttered in the past.

"Then I'll stay as long as you need me," she said, "but I'll need your help, too. I know nothing about running a farmhouse."

When that was settled Buck stretched and yawned. "If you don't need me here tonight I think I'll go on home."

Coralie nodded. "You do look tired. By all means go home and go to bed. We'll be just fine."

He still seemed concerned. "You can call me anytime during the night. My number's pasted on the telephone in the kitchen, and I can get here almost immediately from my house."

"I'll call you if we need you," she said reassuringly, "but Jim will be okay. I'll take good care of him, I promise."

"Aw, I never doubted that." His tone was apologetic. "But you need some rest, too."

She appreciated his concern for her. "I'm an expert at catnapping. I can doze off for fifteen minutes or half an hour and wake up feeling bright and cheerful." She raised her voice slightly. "If I should feel tired I'll ask Gloria for help. She's a very capable young woman."

Coralie watched Gloria out of the corners of her eyes, and knew that she'd heard. Although the girl continued to watch television she sat up straighter and held her head high.

Was it too much to hope that a little praise was all Jim's daughter needed to make her less hostile?

As Buck prepared to leave through the back door Coralie remembered that school was starting up again the next morning and asked Buck what time the girls had to get up, and how they got there.

"Don't worry about that," he told her. "I'll come over early and get 'em up and off. I've got a key so I can let myself in. The school bus picks 'em up about a quarter to eight, but you take care of Jim and let me worry about the kids."

Coralie checked Jim every hour after that, and the girls watched television until ten o'clock. Then she suggested tactfully that they'd better go to bed since they had to get up and go to school early the next morning.

They grumbled, but their arguments were halfhearted, and they did as they were told. It had been a long day and they'd been badly traumatized by their father's injury.

Half an hour later when she no longer heard their footsteps above she went upstairs to find both girls in the twin beds in Gloria's room with the lights out. She thanked them for being so cooperative about the inconvenience of continuing to share the one room and told them good-night.

After taking a long, warm, relaxing shower she put on her nightgown, robe and slippers and went back to check on Jim. It wasn't time to waken him again, but she'd been upstairs in the shower for some time and wanted to be sure he hadn't called to her when she couldn't hear him.

The blinds were open, and the full moon casting its glow on the snow illuminated the room so that she didn't need to turn on the light. She walked to the bed and stood at the side, looking down at him.

His breathing was deep and regular, but he wasn't asleep. His eyes were open and he was watching her. "Oh, I'm sorry," she said tremulously. "I didn't mean to wake you...."

"You didn't," he answered huskily. "I've been lying here waiting for you. There are no nosy nurses around to forbid it, so come to bed with me. I'm not going to let you sit up all night watching me breathe. I'd much rather hold you in my arms and savor your soft warm body against mine. I guarantee you'll be able to keep track of my heartbeat just fine."

Chapter Nine

It never occurred to Coralie to say no to Jim. Instead, she unzipped her robe and stepped out of it, then kicked off her slippers and walked around the bed to crawl in on the other side. His welcoming arms received her and she snuggled against him with her head on his shoulder.

The bed was warm from his body heat, and she could feel his heart beating against her breast. He was right. She could keep much better track of his vital signs from this position.

A moan of contentment escaped Jim's throat as he wrapped Coralie in his embrace. God, but she felt good! Even better than he remembered, and he'd have said that was impossible. She was still damp from the shower, and her long blond hair spilled around her shoulders in sensual disarray. He combed his fingers through it and it wrapped itself around his hands with a life of its own.

"Have you any idea how badly I've wanted to hold you just like this?" he asked softly.

"No," she said against his neck, "but I know how badly I've wanted you to."

A wave of pleasure washed over him, and he could almost forget the pounding pain in his head. "Then why were you going to leave me this morning?"

Her soft hand settled on his chest. "Because you didn't want me to stay."

Every word she said sent a tiny pouf of breath to tickle his neck and send prickles down his spine.

"I've been an idiot," he confessed. "Why didn't you let me know you wanted to?"

"Pride. I've been an idiot, too." Her confession was punctuated by a touch of her lips to his throat. His arms tightened around her, and if he'd been a cat he would have purred.

He rubbed his hands over her back. The flannel nightgown she wore felt soft and clung lightly to his touch. He marveled at the symmetry of her beautifully rounded body. Although she didn't mention it he'd noticed that she was careful about what she ate, avoiding starches, sweets and fried foods. If she worried about her weight she shouldn't.

His roaming hands told him she was as beautifully contoured as she looked. Her broad shoulders tapered down to a small waist, then flared into hips and buttocks designed to entice a man to madness and beyond.

Reluctantly, he moved his hands back to her waist. He had no intention of seducing her. With the throbbing ache in his head and ankle he probably couldn't perform even if he tried, but sex wasn't what he needed from her tonight. He needed her compassion and her loving warmth. Her tenderness and her willingness to give of herself to sooth his hurts, whether physical or emotional.

"Now that we're no longer strangers would you be willing to stay here for the reason you came in the first place?" he asked against her hair. "So we can get to know each other better?"

Her hand was skimming slowly over his shoulder and chest, making his heart pound faster. "It seems to me we know each other pretty well already," she said with a touch of amusement as one of his hands brushed the side of her breast. It was full and firm, and the downy flannel covering it added a delightful extra sensual dimension.

"You have a point there," he quipped, and he wasn't talking about the point of her breast, the nipple, that hardened between his gently flexing fingers. "But not as well as I'd like. Besides, you can't go away without even seeing the community of Copper Canyon, or meeting any of its residents."

He moved his hand back to her waist and tried for a lighter tone because he was aroused. He hadn't intended that, and neither did he welcome it. More than anything he didn't want to frighten her into getting out of bed!

She toyed with one of the buttons on his pajama coat until she got it undone, then slid her hand under it to rest on his bare chest. With a quick intake of breath he put his own hand on top of hers to hold it there, unable to bear the thought of her taking it away.

"Gloria won't like it if I don't leave as soon as you're up and about," Coralie said.

Jim knew she was probably right, but he didn't want to face that problem at the moment. "She and Amber will start school again tomorrow, so they won't be around much," he said offhandedly. "Gloria's at a difficult age and a little prickly, but she'll get over it."

Coralie wasn't so sure, and it worried her that Jim apparently didn't recognize his elder daughter's "prickly" personality as a potential barrier to any relationship Coralie and Jim might want to have in the future.

She wasn't going to burden him with her uneasiness tonight, though. Instead, she sighed and moved to kiss the hollow at the base of his throat. "I'd like to stay for a while longer," she confessed, "but we'll talk about it when you're feeling better. Do you need more pain pills?"

He kissed the top of her head. "No, I don't like being all doped up. I just want to lie here for the rest of the night with you in my arms and watch you sleep."

It thrilled her when he talked like that. She curled up in his embrace, whispered good-night and in minutes was sound asleep.

Coralie woke several times during the night just long enough to recognize that Jim was breathing normally and sleeping soundly. The last time it happened she heard Buck's pickup drive into the barnyard and stop. A glance at the lighted digital alarm clock told her it was five-thirty, and she slid carefully out of bed and hurried up to her own room before Buck came into the house.

Dressing quickly in her usual jeans and sweatshirt she went back downstairs to find Buck in the kitchen making coffee.

"How's Jimmy?" he asked before he even said hello.

"He's fine," she said reassuringly. "He slept through the night without needing more medication. I checked on him just before you came and he's dozing peacefully."

"Oh, thank God," Buck said with a deep sigh of relief. "You think he'll be okay now?"

She smiled. "I'm sure of it. He won't feel too great for a couple of days, and that sprained ankle will make it painful to walk, but he'll be fine."

She looked at the big old schoolroom-type clock on the wall. "If you'd like to start breakfast I'll get the girls up."

"Sure," Buck said and reached for the trusty cast-iron skillet. Coralie wondered if it would be possible for her to convince this family to eat more grains and fruit for breakfast and cut back on the fat, but dismissed the thought. She was their guest, not their nutritionist.

Upstairs, the door to Gloria's room was open so she called cheerfully from the doorway, "Time to wake up, ladies.

Your enforced vacation's over, and the school bus will be here before you know it."

They only snuggled deeper into their blankets and pulled the sheets over their heads.

"Hey, come on now," she said as she walked into the room. "It's after six and Grandpa's fixing breakfast. You don't want to miss the bus."

"Yuck," muttered Amber, but she lowered the sheet and turned over.

Gloria lowered her sheet, opened one eye and moaned. "It's still dark outside."

"Of course it is. It's wintertime, but it'll be light by the time you get dressed. Do you have to fix lunches?"

Amber sat up. "No, we eat in the school cafeteria. I think I'll wear my blue corduroy slacks and my 'Lion King' sweatshirt," she mused.

Gloria sat up and ran her hands through her disheveled hair. "Why don't you throw that old thing out?" she said waspishly. "You've worn it so much that it's all faded."

"I like it," Amber snapped. "It's my very favorite. I suppose you're going to wear that tacky old 'Star Trek' shirt."

"I'm not going to school," Gloria announced dramatically. "I'm going to stay home today and take care of Dad." She turned her head to look at Coralie. "How is he this morning?"

Coralie tried to hide her surprise and dismay by taking a deep breath before she spoke. "Your father is much better. I doubt that he'll want you to miss school. Hurry and get dressed now, both of you, or your breakfast will get cold."

She turned and walked out of the room, hoping Jim wouldn't let Gloria use him as an excuse to stay home when it wasn't necessary.

She stopped in her own room to apply a touch of lipstick and eye makeup, then unpacked her suitcase and put her clothes away before she went back downstairs.

In the kitchen she was surprised to see Jim sitting at the table, nursing a mug of coffee. He was dressed in jeans and a plaid flannel shirt with a slipper on one foot. The other one, which was heavily wrapped in an Ace bandage, wore a thick sock. The cane he'd been given at the hospital was propped by his chair.

He looked up when she came in and she frowned. "Jim, what are you doing out of bed and wandering around?"

She walked over to him and put the back of her hand on his cheek as her gaze searched his face. "Does your head still hurt? Do you feel dizzy?"

He put his arm around her waist and drew her close. "I got out of bed and came in here hoping to find a cup of coffee . . . and you." His tone was innocent, but his deeper meaning was clear. He'd expected to find her in bed beside him when he woke up. "Yes, my head hurts, and, no, I don't feel dizzy. Anything else you'd like to know before I give you a good-morning kiss?"

Startled, she darted a guilty glance toward Buck, but he was standing at the stove with his back to them. She leaned down and brushed her lips against Jim's, intending only a quick buss, but he cupped her head with his hands and expertly explored her mouth.

Her knees almost buckled, and she grabbed his shoulders and hung on as her tongue responded to his.

It was the sound of footsteps tumbling down the stairs that caused them to spring apart. Coralie jumped and made it to the sink before Gloria and Amber came bustling into the kitchen.

They both ran to their dad and hugged him. Coralie saw Jim wince at their enthusiastic but rough handling, and she had to bite her lip to keep from reprimanding them. After all, they were his daughters. If he wanted them to leave him alone he'd tell them so.

"Daddy, are you all well now?" "Does your head still hurt?" "Can you walk okay?" Their questions came thick and fast, interrupting each other without waiting for an answer as the girls hugged and jostled him painfully.

It was Buck who put a stop to it. "Hey, kids, don't be so rowdy!" he bellowed. "You're hurtin' your dad. Be a little careful how you handle him."

They quieted down immediately and moved away from Jim. "I'm sorry, Dad," Gloria apologized. "I didn't think—"

"I'm sorry, too," Amber interrupted contritely. "I didn't mean—"

Jim reached out to both of them and set them on his lap, one on each leg, then wrapped an arm around each child. "It's all right," he assured them. "You didn't know, and besides, it's not every day I get hugged by two beautiful women. I feel fine, but it will take a little while for my head and ankle to heal."

He gave them a cheeky grin. "Meanwhile, I get to sit around the house and watch soap operas while you two are slaving away in school."

"That's not fair," Amber whined teasingly. "You have all the luck."

Jim chuckled. "Thanks a lot, kid," he groused.

"I'm not going to school," Gloria said with quiet confidence, startling them all. "I'm going to stay home and take care of you."

Jim looked at her, but it was a moment before he spoke. "I appreciate the offer, honey, but that's not necessary. Coralie is here to help me if I need it."

Gloria wasn't about to be put off. "Oh, she can straighten up the house and cook the meals, but you need me to take care of you."

Coralie blinked in astonishment. She'd just been insulted, and she didn't believe for a minute that Gloria hadn't known what she was doing.

There was a moment of hushed silence until Jim caught his breath. "Coralie is not a housekeeper, Gloria, she's a nurse. She knows how to care for sick and injured people. That's what she's here for. Now sit down and eat your breakfast."

Gloria pouted, but didn't argue further. Coralie, however, was still stinging. Not only from the girl's remarks, but from Jim's reply.

She knows how to care for sick and injured people. That's what she's here for.

Had he forgotten their conversation of last night so quickly? He'd asked her to stay so they could get to know each other better. The implication had been that he might make her his mail order wife, after all. At least that's the way she'd understood it.

But this morning he told Gloria she was only here for her nursing skills, which would mean that she'd leave as soon as those skills were no longer needed. Why did he deliberately mislead his daughter?

Was it possible that blow on the head had done more damage than she and the doctor had thought? Was Jim having trouble with his short-term memory?

The thought terrified her. Maybe she'd misunderstood his intentions last night. Or, God forbid, maybe because of her close personal feelings for him she was missing symptoms she should be catching because she didn't want to see them.

The custom of medical people not taking care of their own loved ones was a sound one. They couldn't be as objective as they needed to be.

Glancing around the room she noticed that Jim was talking to his girls at the table, and Buck was busy cooking at the stove. She slipped unobtrusively out and went up to her room where she could be alone to think.

As she paced back and forth her thoughts kept returning to her possible incompetency. Was she missing something about Jim's medical condition? Should she suggest that the doctor do a complete physical again? If she asked him to repeat tests she'd have to explain why. That would mean telling Dr. Sam the complete and unabridged history of her brief relationship with Jim.

But Dr. Sam was not only Jim's doctor, he was also his best friend. Would Jim resent her telling his good buddy about the mail order bride debacle? It sounded so tacky, and it put Buck in a bad light, as well as Coralie and Jim.

Jim was very protective of his father, and neither of them would forgive her if she made them look foolish in the eyes of their friends and then it turned out that she'd simply misunderstood Jim's invitation to stay for a while.

On the other hand if there was a complication from the head injury and she didn't report her suspicion it would not only mean the end of her career, but she'd never forgive herself.

A knock on the door caught her attention, and Amber's voice called, "Coralie, I've been looking all over for you. Grandpa says breakfast's ready."

"Okay, honey, I'll be right down," she called back, even though she'd lost her appetite. But neither did she want people questioning her about why she wasn't eating.

Later, when the school bus came, Gloria again pleaded with Jim to let her stay home with him, but once more he refused. By that time he looked exhausted, and Coralie could see the lines of pain around his mouth and eyes.

"It's time for your morning nap," she told him as he limped back into the house, leaning heavily on his cane, after waving goodbye to the girls. Buck had disappeared into the barn.

Jim had one arm around her waist to help balance him. "Are you going to nap with me?" he asked hopefully. "You were gone when I woke up this morning."

"I left your room when I heard Buck drive up," she explained. "After all, you wouldn't want him to find us in bed together."

"Not if it would bother you," Jim said.

That was an odd answer. Did it mean he wouldn't mind if his father knew they'd shared the same bed? On the other hand he'd been quick enough to assure his daughter that Coralie was only the nurse.

She knew she shouldn't bring the subject up now when he was tired and uncomfortable, but she had to know where she stood. She helped him walk into the bedroom, then straightened the bedding and tucked him under the covers.

When she leaned over to pull up the blanket he pulled her down to kiss her. She hadn't intended to let that happen again until she'd had a talk with him, but once their lips met, and fused, she was powerless to stop it and melted against him.

When they finally came up for air he murmured against her mouth. "Lie with me again. At least until I doze off. Dad won't come into the bedroom."

She wanted to curl up in bed with him more than anything, but her innate caution, plus her schooling in medical ethics, helped her to resist.

She kissed him once more lightly, then pulled out of his embrace and sat up on the side of the bed. "I'd like to, Jim, but as long as I'm working as your nurse that type of behavior is highly unprofessional."

He looked confused. "Working as my nurse? Is that all I am to you? A patient?"

He sounded so hurt that she wanted to sink back into his arms and beg him to forget everything she'd said. But, of course, that would defeat the necessity of having to hurt him in the first place.

"No, of course it's not," she assured him, "but I do have a question for you. Do you remember what you asked me last night after we were in bed?"

He frowned. "I seem to remember asking you several things."

"I mean about my staying on here."

"Well, sure. I asked if you'd be willing to stay for a while longer instead of leaving right away as you'd planned."

She perked up. He remembered that right! "Why did you want me to stay?"

"Honey, what are you getting at?" he asked, obviously puzzled. "I asked you to stay so we could get to know each other better. According to both you and Buck that's the reason you came here in the first place. Is something wrong?"

Thank God, at least she didn't have to worry that his injury had affected his memory. He knew pretty much exactly what they'd said during their pillow talk.

"Not really," she said in answer to his question. "I just wondered why you told Gloria I was only here to act as your nurse."

He put his hand to his head and groaned. "Oh, hell, I didn't mean it that way. I was just explaining why I wouldn't let her stay home from school to take care of me. I didn't want to hurt her feelings, but I sure didn't mean to hurt yours, either. I guess that crack on the head jumbled my brain."

She leaned down and kissed him again, delighted to have that cleared up, but feeling a little foolish, too. "No, it didn't. I'm just being overly sensitive. I'm still so embarrassed about having answered an ad for a mail order bride. It was so unlike me. I don't know what I was thinking about."

He reached up and stroked her cheek. "I apologize for my dad's part in that, but I'm glad you did. Otherwise, we'd never have met. Who knows, maybe it was ordained by fate."

"No, it was ordained by Buck," she said as she took his hand and kissed his palm, then stood. "But I'm glad, too. Now go to sleep. Do you need another pain pill?"

He smiled sleepily. "No, I won't have trouble sleeping, but it would be a lot more pleasurable if you'd come to bed with me."

She thought so, too, and for that reason she beat a hasty retreat before she could give in to the temptation.

Jim healed fast, and within two days he was hobbling around the barnyard without his cane, trying to make himself useful. The sun had been out and most of the ice on the ground and roads had melted and dried up. Still, Coralie worried. Dr. Sam had told him to stay off the sprained ankle, but Jim paid no attention.

"There's work to be done, honey," he'd said when she fussed at him about it, "and the two farmhands who work full-time for us in the summer have jobs at one of the nearby ski resorts during the winter. I'm not going to let Buck work himself to death doing the jobs of two husky men just because I've got a sore ankle."

She knew it was useless to argue, so she came up with a different idea. On Thursday night, after Buck had gone home and the girls were in bed, she and Jim were sitting cuddled up together on the sofa watching television when she broached the subject.

"Jim, tomorrow morning you have an appointment to see Dr. Sam for a checkup at his office. I'd like to go with you. I've never seen Copper Canyon except for the hospital."

"That's right, you haven't," he said. "Sure, you can go with me. Be happy for the company." He squeezed her hand.

"And afterward can we have lunch at a restaurant, and then drive around sight-seeing until its time to pick the kids up after school?" She knew she was pushing it.

He was silent for a moment. "Gee, Coralie, I don't know. We're pretty far behind on the work around the farm, and I hate to leave Buck to do it by himself."

She knew she sounded selfish, but if Jim didn't stay off his foot more it might leave permanent damage.

"Why don't you suggest he take the day off, too," she said. "He probably has places he'd like to go and things he'd like to do. The break would do you both good. The girls and I can help with the work around the farm over the weekend. We're all three strong and healthy."

"Oh, no," Jim exclaimed. "The last time I let you help outside you were a basket case by noon."

She wrinkled her nose at him. "Yeah, but I'm a lot smarter for that experience. This time I'll pace myself better. After all, as you told Gloria, I'm not here as your housekeeper."

"You're not here as my farmhand, either," he quipped, "but you're right, I'm not being a very good host. If you want to 'do' the village of Copper Canyon I'll take you on the grand tour."

The following morning was bright and sunny again, and Coralie dressed in the blue slacks suit she'd worn on the airplane and a coat she'd borrowed from Gloria. She hadn't brought many clothes with her, and most of what she had was unsuitable for the Idaho weather and the Buckley lifestyle. It was obvious that she was not a seasoned traveler.

Buck was delighted with the prospect of a day all to himself and announced that he was going into town to get a haircut. According to Jim the local barber shop was a hangout for the older men of the community. They gossiped, swapped stories and discussed the latest news.

"Most of the young people leave here when they get out of school nowadays," he told her, "but the older ones were born here and will die here. Dad's known most of his cronies all his life."

"How come you and Dr. Sam came back after you completed your educations?"

"We had family businesses to come back to," he answered. "Mine was the farm, and Sam took over his dad's medical practice."

"His father was a physician, too?"

Jim nodded. "Yeah. He was the typical country doctor. Delivered both Sam and me just three days apart."

That surprised Coralie. "He delivered his own son?"

Jim shrugged. "He was the only doctor in town, and Eloise, his wife, never had more than a couple of hours of labor with any of her four babies."

Jim's appointment with Sam was for ten o'clock, and Sam's car pulled into the small parking lot right behind theirs.

"Oversleep?" Jim teased Sam as the three of them walked together to the brick building.

"I wish," Sam grumbled. "I just came from the hospital after waiting around since four o'clock for Janet Foster's baby son to put in an appearance."

"Are Janet and the baby okay?" Jim asked with concern.

"Oh, yeah," Sam assured him, "but I don't think she's going to want to go through that again for a while."

Inside the structure they walked down a short hall and entered a suite of rooms near the end. The door had Sam's name on it. A receptionist greeted them, and Sam turned to Coralie. "I want to talk to you first." His glance shifted to Jim. "Alone."

"Hey, that's my woman," Jim bellowed playfully. "You can get one of your own."

Sam grinned. "Afraid I'll steal her away from you?"

Jim's teasing expression faltered a little. "I guess I am. I had to get knocked unconscious to get her to stay with me in the first place. She's hell-bent on going to her family in South Dakota."

There was a short awkward silence until his face split into a big smile. "Oh, well, what the hey. I'll give you five minutes, but don't forget, it was me you had the appointment with."

Sam laughed. "Ah, but she's a nurse. I've got plenty of patients, but we never have enough nurses around here. Maybe I can talk her into staying and working for me."

"In your dreams, buddy," Jim called after them as Sam ushered Coralie into his office.

Sam closed the door and motioned for her to sit down. He took the chair behind the desk and cleared his throat. All trace of joviality were gone. "How's Jim coming along? Since I haven't heard from you I assume he's doing all right?" It was more of a question than a statement.

She sighed. "All his vital signs are normal and he never complains about pain or dizziness, but he won't stay off that foot. He won't even use his cane. Neither will he slow down and take it easy. The best I can manage is to get him to take a short nap in the afternoon."

Sam shook his head. "Knowing Jim that's more than any of the rest of us could have done. Are you sure there's no residual pain or dizziness from the head wound?"

She shook her head. "No, I'm not. In fact I'm almost sure there is. Sometimes when he doesn't know I'm watching I can see it in his expression or gestures, but he won't admit it. He won't take the pain pills you gave him, either."

Sam grimaced. "That's our Jim. He's always there to help when someone needs him, but he'll never admit that once in a while he needs someone, too. All I can suggest is that you keep a close eye on him and report to me immediately if he exhibits any symptoms that worry you. How much longer will you be here?"

She didn't know what to say. She couldn't stay much longer without raising a lot of questions in everyone's mind. Also, the sexual tension between herself and Jim was getting awfully close to out of control. She knew better than to get intimately involved unless he asked her to marry him, but the longer she remained the harder it got to resist the powerful attraction that vibrated between them.

"I'll stay as long as he needs me—that is, as long as he needs my nursing expertise," she corrected herself. "I guess that will be up to you."

Sam hesitated, as if he wanted to say something but wasn't sure he should. He must have decided against it because when he spoke it was just a simple observation. "I see. Well, as far as his physical condition is concerned you can leave anytime you want to. You and he will have to work that out by yourselves."

Coralie shivered. In other words, she wasn't going to get any help from Sam in deciding how long she'd give Jim to make up his mind whether or not he wanted her!

As soon as Coralie returned to the waiting room Sam's nurse summoned Jim. She led him to an examining room and told him to take the shoe off his injured foot and pull his pants leg up as high as it would go. He complained good-naturedly as she unwound the Ace bandage and took it off.

It was only a few minutes after she left that Sam came in. Jim was always glad to see his close friend, and they bantered breezily while Sam examined Jim's head and ankle.

When he was finished he took off his gloves and tossed them into a waste receptacle. "You've got the hardest damn head I ever saw," he groused. "Anyone else would have cracked their skull on that sharp concrete step, but you . . ." He rolled his eyes. "You hardly miss a beat. You better start being a little careful, Jim boy. One of these days that luck of yours is bound to change."

Jim guffawed. "Aw, come off it. You're just jealous because I've got a good nurse."

Sam sobered. "Yeah, you're right, I am. You want to tell me about Coralie? Where she came from, and where this relationship is leading? She's pretty young. Are you sure you know what you're doing?"

If any other man had questioned him Jim would have taken offense, but he and Sam had been sharing confidences all their lives. It was a relief to have him to talk to.

Jim told him about Buck's effort to get his son a mail order wife, and all the upheaval and misunderstanding it caused. "I was upset, but had to bring her home with me," he explained. "She was my responsibility and I couldn't leave her stranded in that airport for God only knows how many days."

Sam chuckled. "I'd never have believed Buck would do such a thing. Whatever made him think you needed a wife that bad?"

"Who knows?" Jim said grimly. "I haven't made any secret of the fact that another wife is the last thing I need or want."

"So what happened after you took her home?"

"We got snowed in," Jim answered and told him about his family's forced confinement in the house during the storm, Gloria's animosity toward Coralie and Coralie's decision to leave as soon as the roads were opened. "We were just getting into the car to go to the airport when I twisted my ankle and slipped on the ice. Since then she's been indispensable."

Sam cleared his throat. "You mean as a nurse? A housekeeper? Or a lover?"

Jim felt a jab of irritation. "We're not sleeping together," he said sharply.

"Then what's the problem?"

Jim's irritation intensified. "What makes you think there's a problem?" His tone was gruff.

"Oh, come on, man, I'm trained to be observant. I've seen the looks you two exchange, and you can't keep your hands off her. Also, I haven't noticed her objecting."

Jim relaxed. He sometimes forgot that his good buddy was a top-notch physician whose business it was to contemplate and understand human behavior.

"You're right. She's driving me crazy," he admitted.

"Then you're either going to have to marry her or send her away."

A weight settled in Jim's stomach. "Thanks a bunch, pal," he said sarcastically. "I'd never have figured that out by myself."

Sam didn't react to the taunt. "So have you decided yet which it's going to be?"

Jim's temper was rising. "I don't have any choice. She's much too young, she's a city girl who's never been on a farm before, we have almost nothing in common and the girls don't want her for a stepmother. I'd be courting disaster if I let myself fall in love with her. She'd eventually leave the same way Marsha did, and I couldn't go through that again. I'm going to send her away."

Sam nodded. "In that case I suggest that you do it soon, Jimmy. Frankly, I'm afraid you're already too late."

Chapter Ten

For once Jim had no snappy comeback. Neither of them spoke again, but Dr. Sam's ominous words rang in Jim's ears as Sam ushered him out into the reception room where Coralie was waiting.

He hadn't had to ask Sam what he meant. That same thought had been hiding just below the surface of his heart and mind since he came to in the hospital and found Coralie hovering over the bed. Even in his confused state his relief at seeing her there had been enormous, but also troubling.

He hadn't wanted her to be that important to him. He still didn't, but the very thought of sending her away was too painful to contemplate.

Was Sam right? Was it already too late to keep himself from falling in love with her?

In the reception room Coralie put down the magazine she'd been skimming and looked at her watch. Jim had been with the doctor for nearly forty-five minutes. Surely it shouldn't take so long just to examine his head and ankle.

She fidgeted uncomfortably, but a few minutes later the door opened and Jim came out, followed by Sam. She stood and at first glance Jim looked thoughtful, almost rebellious, but when he saw her he grinned and put his arm around her. "Doc here says I'm good as new," he announced triumphantly.

"And God should strike you dead for lying," Sam scolded.

He looked at Coralie. "Jim's coming along nicely, *but—*" he strongly emphasized the word "—he's to stay off that foot as much as possible until the swelling goes down, and he's to tell you truthfully when his head hurts and how much."

Sam's professional demeanor changed to a smile. "You have my permission to chain him to a chair if he doesn't follow my orders."

She laughed. "Believe me, that's exactly what I'll do, too."

Jim hugged her to his side. "Smarty pants," he muttered. "Who do you think you're kidding? You know I'm putty in your pretty little hands."

Coralie hooted as he turned his attention to Sam. "I'm giving Coralie the fifty-cent tour of Copper Canyon today. How about joining us for lunch? Kathy's Kitchen at twelve-thirty?"

The rest of the day was pure delight. Jim drove slowly around the small town that boasted a population of 3,046 on a sign posted along the highway.

It was a charming snow-covered village with more churches than taverns, and an old-fashioned Main Street that was the heart of the town. Coralie giggled at storefront signs identifying Baldwin's Dry Goods, Ski Emporium, Buzz's Hardware and, of course, Kathy's Kitchen, where they met Sam for lunch.

The meal was home cooked and delicious, but even more enlightening was the reception Jim received from everyone he came in contact with. They all greeted him enthusiastically with a handshake, a punch on the shoulder or a shout from across the room. Most stopped to talk.

He introduced Coralie as a family friend from California, and she learned several surprising things about him that he'd neglected to tell her. Such as that he was president of the school board, an elected member of the county supervisors and a coach of the softball team his daughters played on.

When she chided him for not telling her about all his civic duties he just laughed and said it was all part of being a good citizen, and hopefully assuring his children of a nice, clean, pleasant place to live.

After lunch Sam went back to his office, and Jim took her to see the school his daughters attended. It was a complex of several buildings grouped together where the town children as well as those from the farms in the surrounding area were taught from kindergarten through twelfth grade.

Coralie was fascinated. "I went to three totally different schools all in the same district," she said. "Elementary, middle and high. Every time I'd get used to one I'd be shifted to another and have to start all over again, meeting new kids, learning where things were and what was expected of me."

"That's not necessarily bad, honey," Jim told her. "It prepares you better for the real world than the cloistered setup we have, but I admit our way is less stressful for our kids.

"Oh, I almost forgot to show you our newspaper office."

Her eyes widened as he turned a corner. "Copper Canyon has a newspaper?"

"Damn straight," he chided. "*The Copper Canyon Star Journal*. It's published once a week, and keeps us all up on the latest local news."

Coralie sniffed. "You should save your money. You can get that every day just by walking down Main Street."

When they'd seen all there was of interest in Copper Canyon Jim took her on a self-guided driving tour of the nearby White Bird Battlefield, the sight of the first confrontation of the Nez Percé Indian war.

Coralie wasn't familiar with the history of Idaho, and Jim kept up a running commentary of how, in 1877, the U.S. army tried to relocate the Nez Percé tribe. Their leader, Chief Joseph, led them into battle, and against huge odds the small tribe defeated the U.S. troops at White Bird Canyon. Later the tribe was forced to retreat. It was after that that Chief Joseph gave his famous surrender speech in which he vowed, "I will fight no more forever."

Coralie found it so interesting and asked so many questions that they were almost late getting back to Copper Canyon to pick up Gloria and Amber from school.

Gloria was in a foul mood. She and another girl had gotten into a fight in the hallway and they'd both been punished. She told her dad about it on the drive back to the farm. "It wasn't even my fault," she ranted. "Jenny just came up and tried to grab the papers out of my hand. I had a right to push her away."

"What papers were you carrying?" Jim asked.

"Just some of my stuff," she answered, somewhat evasively it seemed to Coralie.

"Did she fall down when you pushed her?" Jim asked. "Was she hurt?"

"Oh, she's so clumsy she falls over her own feet," Gloria said disdainfully. "She said she hurt her hip, but you could tell she was lying."

What was obvious to Coralie was that Gloria wasn't telling her father everything, and she turned around to look at the two girls sitting in the back seat. "Are you sure? Did the school nurse examine her? She could have cracked a bone—"

Gloria gave her a look filled with disgust. "We don't have a school nurse, and she didn't fall that hard. I hardly tapped her. She fell on purpose."

"All the same," Coralie said anxiously, "she should have been examined—"

Again Gloria interrupted. "Look, I already said she was limping around on purpose. Okay? Besides, I wasn't talking to you so butt out."

This time it was Jim who interrupted. "Oh, for God's sake, cut the bickering," he said impatiently. "Coralie, you weren't there so don't make accusations until you know what you're talking about—"

Coralie was stung by his angry words. "But I wasn't accusing anybody—" she tried to say, but was drowned out when he continued to scold.

"When we get home I'll let you all out and go back to talk to the principal."

"No, Dad, don't do that," Gloria said urgently. "Mrs. Keller doesn't like me. She'll say it was my fault. Jenny's one of her pets."

Coralie was not only hurt but angry that Jim would reprimand her when all she was trying to do was give them the benefit of her training in first aid and emergency procedure.

She recognized a cover-up when she heard one. Gloria must have started the fight and now was trying to weasel out of accepting responsibility. It hadn't been that long ago that Coralie was a teenager. She remembered that some of her friends had gotten around their parents with half truths and exaggerations. She'd even tried it herself once, but her dad and stepmother didn't buy it for a minute.

Gloria was good. She'd certainly gotten all her father's attention, but she might have gone too far this time. She obviously didn't want Jim to talk to the principal.

Jim frowned as he turned into the narrow road that led to the house. "But, honey, if you're being punished for something you didn't do—"

"It's okay, Daddy," she interrupted. "I can handle it. It would just make things worse if you got involved."

Jim parked the Jeep beside the house and opened the door. "Well...if you're sure. But I want you to tell me if this goes any further. Promise?"

She leaned over the back seat and hugged him. "I promise," she said, then opened her door and got out.

Coralie was furious as she stomped up the steps to the porch. Not only had Gloria wrapped her dad around her little finger, but she'd managed to ruin what up to now had been a wonderful day.

It also reminded her of something she'd almost managed to overlook lately. That Gloria could make life miserable for her if she married Jim over his daughter's objections.

Or would it even come to that? If he decided he loved Coralie and wanted to marry her but Gloria objected he'd probably sacrifice his own happiness and Coralie's in order to appease his daughter.

But would that be so bad? He was the girl's father. He was responsible for her well-being, and he felt he had to make up to her for her mother's abandonment.

Coralie strode into the house and went upstairs to her room. She knew that anything she might say now would only make matters worse.

An hour later when it was time to start supper she was still nursing her hurt feelings, but had decided to make a huge effort not to show it. She headed for a stop-off in the bathroom before going downstairs, and as she walked past the open door of Gloria's room she glanced inside. Both girls were there, lying on their beds watching television, and the room looked like a pigsty.

Their slovenly habits had bothered her before. Although she straightened up the rest of the house she refused to clean their room. The clutter had bothered her, but not enough to issue orders to clean it up. Orders she knew would be ignored.

Today, though, she was already upset, and the unsightly, not to mention unsanitary, mess sparked her already churning temper. "For heaven's sake," she said, trying to keep her voice low and reasonably calm. "Why don't you girls clean up this mess? It's actually starting to smell in here."

Both girls looked at her, startled, and Amber sat up, but Gloria lounged across her twin bed and eyed Coralie with bored contempt. "That's your job. You're the housekeeper."

Coralie was incensed. "I am not your housekeeper," she informed the girl icily. "And if I were I'd charge double time to clean up this...this trash heap. It's disgraceful. I'd think you'd have more pride."

That brought Gloria to her feet. "Pride," she blurted. "What do you know about pride? Dad brought you here to wait out the blizzard and now you don't have the good manners to leave." Her voice escalated with every word.

For a moment Coralie was speechless with rage. "I haven't left because your dad and the doctor both asked me not to until Jim was able to get around better," she shouted. "As I remember so did the two of you."

"So what are you still doing here?" Gloria shouted back. "Dad's getting along just fine. We don't need you anymore..."

Neither of them heard Jim until his voice boomed from the stairway. "What in hell is going on up here?"

His face was twisted with anger as he took the steps two at a time. "I could hear you all the way outside!" His voice carried even farther than that and with more authority as he glared at the three of them. "Can't you kids ever learn to get along? What brought this on?"

Coralie gasped. *You kids?* He was lumping her in with his teenage daughters, but before she could protest Gloria spoke.

"Amber and I were just watching television when *she* came in and started hollering at us to clean up our room." Gloria sobbed as tears that hadn't been there seconds before ran down her cheeks.

"That's not—" Coralie started to defend herself, then belatedly realized what was happening. Jim was treating her like one of the kids because she was acting like one. She'd let her hurt feelings and temper get the better of her, but she wasn't going to be sucked into the game of defending accusations by making accusations.

Jim had his arms around Gloria, comforting her, but he glanced at Coralie over her head. There was a question in his eyes, but she didn't know how to answer it without appearing as adolescent as his teenager.

"I... I only asked them to pick up their room," she said quietly. "If you'll excuse me I'll go fix supper."

Without waiting for him to answer she turned and left.

The rest of the evening was strained and tense. Buck had had dinner at noon with friends at a café in town so he didn't come over for the evening meal. At the supper table Amber looked confused, Gloria pouted and Jim tried to soothe things over by ignoring the episode and trying to make light conversation. Coralie pushed food around on her plate and spoke only when spoken to.

When the meal was over, Jim, in an apparent effort to placate Coralie, did insist that the girls do the dishes, but that just brought on another argument between father and daughters and upset Coralie even more. She didn't want to be a cause of dissension between them.

While Amber and Gloria cleaned up the kitchen, under protest, Coralie went upstairs, took her bath and put on her nightie and robe. There was a small television set in her room, and she propped herself up on the bed with pillows and settled back to watch it.

At nine-thirty she heard the girls come upstairs and run the water for their nightly baths, all the while fussing at each other for taking too long and-or using all the hot water. By ten o'clock everything was quiet and she'd just switched on the news when there was a soft knock at the door.

"Coralie," Jim said. "Are you asleep?"

She hated the way her heart raced and her temperature seemed to rise just at the sound of his voice. Her first impulse was to run to the door and open it, or better yet invite him to come in.

Instead, she answered quietly. "No, Jim, I'm not asleep."

"Would you mind coming downstairs? I'd like to talk to you." He sounded anxious.

"Of course," she said primly. "I'll be down in a few minutes."

She dressed hurriedly in clean brown slacks and a matching brown sweater, then ran the brush through her hair. She forced herself to walk slowly down the stairs instead of racing down the way she'd like to. Jim had seen her as an unruly child this afternoon. Tonight she wanted to show him that she could also be a dignified woman.

He was waiting for her in the living room, standing with one foot on the fireplace hearth and his arm across his thigh, looking into the fire. She was wearing a pair of heavy socks but no shoes, and he didn't hear her come in. His shoulders were slumped, and his stance suggested weariness or discouragement.

She ached to reach out to him, to curl up in his arms and forget everything but the yearning to be with him that gnawed at her vitals. Instead, she crossed the room to stand beside him.

He straightened up and put his foot on the floor, then turned his head and looked at her with a sad little smile. "Hello, sweetheart," he murmured softly.

His gentle tone and the sweetness of the endearment melted any residual resistance she may have had, and it took all her willpower to keep her distance and her dignity intact.

"You wanted me?" she asked, and her voice was barely more than a whisper.

"Oh, yes, I want you." The sensual inference in his tone couldn't be missed. "I want you so much that I can't think straight anymore."

She stood still, neither stepping backward nor forward as he raised his hand to cup her chin and lift her face so he could look into her eyes. "I'm sorry, Coralie," he said hoarsely, and his deep brown eyes were filled with regret. "The last thing I'd consciously do is hurt you, not even your feelings."

She pulled her head away from his hand. "My hurt feelings aren't as important as the fact that you made me look like an interloper by criticizing me in front of the girls. I'm not an employee who needs to be reminded of her place."

He looked surprised. "That was never my intention," he protested. "The only excuse I have for blowing up the way I did is because I had a talk with Sam that upset me and—"

A shot of alarm tore through her. "Jim, did he find something wrong when he examined you!" she interrupted anxiously, forgetting both her dignity and her pride as she moved toward him and his arms encircled her in a warm and loving embrace.

"No, love, no. Nothing like that," he assured her calmly as he hugged her to him. "This was a personal conversation we had that had nothing to do with my injuries."

"Are you sure," she pressed, her heart still pounding with fear.

"Very sure," he whispered in her ear. His breath tickled her and made her shiver. "You can call and ask him if it will relieve your mind."

She heard the sincerity in his tone and relaxed into the sheer pleasure of her body melded with his. She put her arms around his neck and sighed as she laid her head on his shoulder.

"It was my fault, too," she admitted. "I was behaving like one of the kids instead of the adult I'm supposed to be. I had no business poking my nose in either time."

"You were only trying to help, and you were right. I *am* too lax with my daughters. They should be responsible for cleaning up their room and helping with the housework, and as for the incident at school—"

Coralie raised her head and leaned back in his embrace, loosening his hold on her. "That's between you, Gloria and the school authorities," she interrupted. "I only wanted to point out that if the girl Gloria pushed was injured you could be sued."

"I know I could," he admitted, "but even more important, if Jenny was injured she should be treated as soon as possible so the injury isn't aggravated. I've already set up an appointment to meet with Hannah Keller tomorrow morning. Do you want to go with me?"

Coralie was surprised that he'd even invite her. "No," she said and pulled away from him. "I assume Ms. Keller is the principal, and my being there would only make Gloria more resentful."

Jim let her go reluctantly. "I suppose you're right, but if you two can't get along . . ." His words trailed off and were left hanging in the air.

"Exactly," she said, fighting to hold back the sob that blocked her throat. "If Gloria won't accept me, then there's no future for you and me. I really think I'd better make arrangements to leave as soon as possible. . . ."

He shook his head urgently and opened his mouth to speak, but she hurried on. "No, please, listen to me. There's a lot of high-tension chemistry between us, we both know that, and we'd just be courting real heartbreak if I stay here where we're living in each other's pockets, so to speak, until our feelings grow even deeper and become impossible to control...."

The sob broke through then, and she turned her back to him in an effort to compose herself.

He didn't allow her that small privacy. Putting his hands on her shoulders he turned her around. "I want you to look at me, sweetheart, and tell me that it will be less painful for you to leave me tomorrow than it would be a week from tomorrow."

His gaze bored into hers and she was caught. With a sinking feeling she knew it was already too late. She'd foolishly let herself fall in love, and now there was no way out.

She felt tears pooling in her eyes and blinked in an effort to keep them from falling as she raised her face to his. "I...I can't tell you such a monstrous lie, Jim. I was determined not to fall in love with you, but I had no choice. Now I'll have to pay the price and it makes no sense to prolong the agony."

She felt a tear trickle down one cheek, and with a groan he gathered her in his arms and held her. "Don't cry, Coralie. I can't resist your tears. I'll do anything you want...."

She sniffled and wiped away the tear. "All I ever wanted from you was for you to love me."

He kissed both of her wet eyelids. "But, darling, you don't have to cry for that. I've loved you right from the start. That's why I was so ticked off by Sam this morning. He's the one who made me face it."

She blinked. "Dr. Sam told you you were in love with me?"

Jim chuckled. "Well, more or less. He's a lot more perceptive than I am."

"And you didn't want to love me?"

"Honey, I didn't want to be in love, period," he said emphatically. "It hurts too damn much. I swore I'd never go through that again."

A twinge of doubt stung her. "Are you still in love with Marsha?"

For a moment he looked as if he hadn't understood the question. Then he shook his head. "No, you don't understand. The passion she and I once shared had languished long before she left. Oh, we went through the motions, even in private, but the slow death of love can be excruciatingly painful. The quarrels, the misunderstandings, the hope that lasted long after there was no spark left to rekindle it..."

He was looking off into space, reliving old pain, and Coralie wished she'd never asked the question.

"No, love, it wasn't Marsha's decision to leave me that I found so difficult to accept, it was the way she did it. I was crushed by the fact that the woman I once thought I knew and loved could have such callous disregard for our children that she could simply walk away from them and never look back."

He managed to focus his attention back on Coralie, and she saw the stark anguish in his eyes. "That's why I never wanted to fall in love again. And now that it's happened much against my will and my better judgment, it terrifies me."

She put out her hand and stroked his cheek. "Do you honestly believe that if we married I might someday leave you and any children we might have?" Her voice shook with emotion.

He put his arms around her and pulled her close. "I don't think you would, no, but I just don't *know*. I didn't think Marsha would, either. There's one thing I do know for sure, though."

She cuddled against him. "And what's that?"

He rubbed his cheek in her hair. "If I ever had you and then lost you I'd never survive. Knowing that, are you willing to gamble on the chance that our marriage could be a happy one even though you had to live on a farm in Idaho and help raise two teenage stepdaughters?"

For just a moment she felt a prickle of doubt, almost a premonition, when he mentioned his children, but she ruthlessly pushed it aside. The one thing she knew for sure was that she could never be happy without Jim. She'd find some way to come to terms with Gloria's almost certain opposition.

She raised her head and looked at him. "I'll not only gamble with you, I'll call you on it and raise you two sons."

His arms tightened around her and his mouth captured hers. After that she had no more uncertainty. She loved Jim and he loved her. They could surmount any obstacle.

Couldn't they?

Coralie woke the following morning with a song in her heart and the rosy picture of a long, gloriously happy future with Jim on her mind. After cuddling up with him on the couch until nearly midnight last night she'd expected to have trouble tempering down her libido enough to sleep, but she'd dozed off almost as soon as she crawled into bed.

They wanted to be married as soon as possible, but both agreed it would be best to postpone announcing their engagement to the family for a few days until the timing was right. Buck, of course, would be delighted, and Amber would probably accept it, but Gloria needed special handling.

A glance out the window told her the weather wasn't as bright as her dreams on this happy morning. It was dark, overcast and starting to snow again.

Downstairs in the kitchen the girls and Buck were finishing breakfast and Jim was apparently still out doing the morning chores. The three at the table looked up when she came in, and Buck beamed his usual happy smile and greeted her. Amber said, "Hello," and Gloria scowled.

"If you don't want to get snowed in again, Coralie," she said, "you'd better make plans to leave as soon as possible. There's another blizzard forecast."

"Gloria!" Buck growled. "Where are your manners? This storm won't be a blizzard, and even if it is Coralie can wait it out with us again."

Gloria looked displeased, but her tone was cordial. "I'm just telling her, Grandpa. The airport's still open, but you know how unreliable our winter storms are."

Coralie didn't know what to say. She couldn't tell the girl that she wasn't going to leave now or ever. This was definitely not the time, and besides, she and Jim had agreed that he would be the one to tell his children about their coming marriage.

She forced a smile. "Thank you, Gloria, I—"

She was saved by the sound of Jim stamping snow off his boots in the porch just before he opened the door and came in.

They had a steamy good-morning embrace as soon as the girls and Buck were out of the house, and she didn't tell him what Gloria had said. She didn't want to cause more trouble, but the glow had been taken off her happiness.

Later that morning when Jim came back from his meeting with the school principal he brought Gloria with him. They were both glowering and Gloria had been crying. Without a word to Coralie Jim ushered his daughter upstairs and into her room.

She found out later what had occurred when Jim came down and sank onto the couch, looking angry and uncertain. "I just don't know," he said when she sat down beside him and asked about his meeting with the school principal. "The two girls have conflicting stories. You heard Gloria's yesterday, but Jenny insists that the papers she tried to get back from Gloria were personal letters to her from her boyfriend that Gloria had found and was reading aloud to another girl in the hallway."

"Did the officials question the other girl?" Coralie asked.

"Yeah. She says the papers were not Jenny's letters, but a friend of Jenny's claims she saw Gloria take the letters from Jenny's desk."

He sighed and ran his fingers through his hair. "I just can't believe Gloria would do such a thing."

Coralie wasn't so sure, and she made the mistake of voicing her doubts. "I don't know, Jim, high school kids tease one another that way, and Gloria was being pretty evasive when you questioned her yesterday."

Jim glared at her. "That's not true," he said angrily. "My daughter wouldn't steal, and she wasn't being evasive. Damn, I didn't expect you to turn on her, too."

Coralie gasped. "Oh, darling, I'm not accusing her of stealing. It was probably just a prank. The type that teenagers play on one another, but this time it got out of hand."

"I don't suppose it has occurred to you that it might be Jenny who is lying?" he said sarcastically.

Coralie didn't know how to answer that without upsetting him further. Instead, she said, "Was Jenny hurt?"

He shrugged. "Her parents took her to their doctor, Sam's associate, and he couldn't find any injury, but she still complained of pain in her hip today so they kept her home from school. Hannah called Gloria into her office and questioned her again, which upset her so that I took her out of school for the rest of the day and brought her home."

He looked so dejected that she put her arms around him in an offer of comfort. She was surprised and hurt when he gently but firmly pulled away from her and stood. "I've got to get back to work," he said and walked away, leaving Coralie bewildered and alone.

Chapter Eleven

For the rest of the day Coralie's mood was as gray as the sky. She and Jim hadn't even had a chance to announce their engagement yet and already they were having trouble. On Monday she'd been mad at Jim, and now, just two days later, he was mad at her, and both of their anger had been triggered by Gloria.

Yesterday she'd been so happy, last night she'd been positively ecstatic and now she was frightened and depressed. Was this a portent of what her life with Jim and his children would be like?

No, she wouldn't allow it! She and Jim loved each other. They could be happy together. They *would* be happy together, she'd see to that. It would just require more effort on her part.

There was no reason why she couldn't get along with Gloria if she just tried harder. Gloria was at a difficult age, and she was a young woman in pain. She'd been rejected by her mother and desperately needed love, but was afraid to reach out for it to anyone but her father. She wanted his

unconditional love, and didn't intend to share it with anybody.

Coralie could understand this, but she had a great deal of
trouble dealing with it. She wanted Jim's unconditional
love, too, and she wasn't sure she could settle for less.

But if she didn't she'd have nothing.

At noon the atmosphere was quiet and gloomy. Gloria
didn't come down to eat. Jim and Buck, who had been told
by his son about Gloria's difficulty at school, ate silently,
and Coralie picked at her food.

Afterward, Jim took a plate up to Gloria and stayed there
for a while, talking to her. When he came back down Coralie was at the sink washing dishes.

He came up behind her and put his arms around her.
"Gloria should be helping you with these," he murmured
and nuzzled the back of her neck.

Then why don't you make her come down here and do it?
she thought resentfully even as she leaned back against him
and tipped her head for more.

"I love you," he whispered, and she capitulated. Turning in his arms she kissed him and whispered back, "I love
you, too."

Jim went out to the barn then to prepare the animals for
the predicted storm, and a short time later Gloria came
downstairs and confronted Coralie.

"Well, I hope you're happy now," she lashed out angrily
as she flounced into the kitchen where Coralie was putting
dishes away. "You managed to get me in trouble."

Coralie wasn't used to being attacked with unjust accusations and her first impulse was to fight back, but she knew
that would be a mistake. Instead, she swallowed a sharp re-
tort and turned to face the girl. "I didn't get you in trouble, Gloria." Her tone was reasonably calm.

"Oh, yes, you did," Gloria snapped. "You had to butt in
and show off how smart you are, and now the principal and

all the parents are involved. Why don't you go back to where you came from and leave us alone!''

Coralie honestly couldn't remember ever having so much antagonism directed at her before. She'd always gotten along with people, even those she didn't especially like, but this half child-half woman managed to pique the temper she hadn't known she had almost every time they were together.

Again she fought for control. ''What did you expect when you knocked that other girl down? Surely you knew an attack like that would have to be investigated.''

''I didn't attack her!'' Gloria raged as her tone escalated. ''She attacked me. I just pushed her away, and now you've got everyone thinking it was my fault.''

Coralie bristled and her voice also rose. ''I had nothing to do with it, as you very well know. You'd better get your act together, young lady, and accept the responsibility for your own actions instead of blaming everyone else. If Jenny has a lasting injury because of this your dad could be sued!''

Coralie immediately regretted that last sentence, especially when she saw the fear that leapt into Gloria's eyes. Coralie didn't want to scare or threaten her. She just wanted to make her understand the possible consequences of her aggressive behavior.

Gloria's face turned red. ''There! You see!'' she yelled, her voice shrill with rage. ''You think I'm lying, and you'll go straight to Dad and tell him so!''

Coralie opened her mouth to reply, but Jim's commanding voice cut through the vibrating second of silence.

''Gloria! Coralie! What's the matter with you two? You behave like a couple of spitting cats. What is it Coralie's going to tell me about?''

Both Coralie and Gloria jumped and turned toward him. Neither of them had heard him come in, and the look of thunder on his face was definitely intimidating.

''Daddy!'' Gloria said. ''I didn't hear you—''

"Well, I heard you. Both of you, and I'm getting tired of having to mediate your battles. Can't we have a little peace around here?"

He turned to Gloria. "What is it you're afraid Coralie's going to tell me?" he demanded again.

Gloria's dark eyes, so like Jim's, filled with tears, but this time they weren't forced. Coralie had no doubt that she was genuinely upset and apprehensive.

"She . . . she thinks I'm lying about what happened with Jenny," Gloria stammered. "She just wants to cause trouble."

Jim looked at Coralie, and she saw the accusation in his eyes even though he didn't voice it. "Is that true?"

The first statement was true, and she had good reason to think that, but the way father and daughter glared at her made her cringe and feel guilty. At this moment they were locked in battle against her, and she couldn't answer without either lying or incriminating herself. If she tried to explain it would put her on the defensive, and she had nothing to be defensive about.

She couldn't meet Jim's gaze. The reproach in it was too painful. Instead, she looked at his chest, and that reminded her how muscular and comforting it felt when he held her against it.

She had unshed tears, too, but she wasn't going to let him see them. She just hoped she wouldn't sob when she tried to speak. "I . . . I think she's not telling you everything," she said hesitantly.

Gloria sobbed, and Jim reached out and cradled her in his arms. "What makes you think that?"

The question was the toll of a death knell to all of Coralie's glowing hopes and plans for a future with this man. It would never work out. Marriage for them would be a disaster, so she might as well speak up about Gloria's problem. Maybe in the long run it would even help.

She lifted her chin, looked him in the eye and told him exactly what she'd said only minutes before to Gloria. The girl cried all the while Coralie was talking and it was evident that Jim wasn't taking her criticism or her well-meant advice at all well. His mouth was set in a grim line, and the accusation in his eyes turned to chilling disbelief.

"I'm sorry Gloria was rude to you," he said when she'd finished, "but you knew how upset she's been over this incident. Why didn't you come to me with your doubts and suspicions? Or better yet, wait until the matter was investigated and the truth arrived at instead of accosting her now with your unfounded inferences and recriminations?"

It was like a brisk slap in the face to Coralie. Jim had made it abundantly plain that if she fought either or both of his daughters for his attention she'd lose. He claimed to love her, but she could see that she'd always be an "also ran" in the order of family members who were important to him.

The hopelessness of the situation washed over Coralie, and she blinked back the tears that burned her eyes. She wished she could afford the luxury of a good cry, too, but it was his daughter he held in his arms, not her. Not the woman he'd just last night asked to spend the rest of her life with him as his wife.

"In other words, it's none of my business so butt out," she said. "Well, for once I agree. Now if you'll excuse me I have things to do."

He looked staggered, but she turned and with her head high and her gait steady she walked out of the room and up the stairs, all the while blinded by tears and praying she wouldn't stumble and fall flat on her face.

Coralie had bathed her face and applied makeup to hide the ravages of her crying spell, then changed her clothes and was nearly finished packing when there was a knock on her bedroom door and Jim's voice called, "Coralie. May I come in?"

She wasn't up to facing him yet, but she had to do it soon so it might as well be now. "Yes, Jim."

The door opened and he stepped inside. "Honey, don't hide away up here. I'm so sorry—"

He caught his breath when he saw the nearly packed suitcase open on the bed. "What are you doing?" There was an undercurrent of fear in his tone.

She didn't turn around to look at him, but continued to sort out her clothes. "I'm packing."

"Packing?" He sounded as if he didn't understand the word. "But why?"

"So I can take my clothes with me when I leave."

"Leave!" The fear in his voice escalated. "Coralie, be reasonable. Where are you going?"

She still kept her back to him. "I'm going to ask Buck to drive me to a motel in Copper Canyon. I'll spend the night there, and in the morning I'll inquire about finding a ride to the airport in Lewiston."

She straightened up then and turned to face him. He looked as if he'd been poleaxed. Surely he must have known that marriage was impossible for them after that scene downstairs.

"I'm going to South Dakota where I should have gone as soon as the roads were opened."

"No!" he said urgently and cupped her shoulders with his hands. "Sweetheart, don't do this to me. I'm sorry for the way I talked to you downstairs. I didn't mean... I lost my temper and lashed out.... It won't happen again, I promise."

His hands on her shoulders were warm and comforting, and she wanted to believe him. To be able to relax and let him hold her, but she couldn't. "It would happen again, Jim. Your first duty is to your children, and I guess I'm not mature enough to be the stepmother of teenagers. It would never work. Now, please, will you find Buck for me?"

He shook his head. "No. If you insist on going into town I'll go with you. We don't have any privacy here. We can spend the night alone together and try to settle our differences. I'm not going to let you get away from me, sweetheart. I love you."

Coralie shivered. She wished he wouldn't talk like that. Especially not about spending the night together. That invitation was almost impossible to resist. She wanted him so badly!

Turning from him again she put some space between them. Apparently, he thought that making love would magically solve all their problems. If only that were true.

"I'm not going to sleep with you, Jim." Her voice was raspy with anguish.

"All right," he said. "I didn't mean that to be an assumption. We'll get separate rooms, but we have to talk—"

"I'm afraid we've talked too much already," she said sadly. "If you don't understand by now the staggering obstacles to our finding happiness together you will when you've had time to think about it. You can blame me. I'm selfish. I want to be as important to you as your daughters are."

Jim looked as tormented as she felt. "Coralie, don't make me choose between you and my children," he said raggedly. It wasn't a demand but a desperate plea.

His pain, mingled with her own, was almost more than she could bear. "Oh, my darling, I'd never do that." Her voice was raw with pain. "Don't you see? That's why I'm not giving you a choice. There is no alternative. I have to leave. Please don't make it any harder for me than it already is."

Chapter Twelve

Winner, South Dakota
Six weeks later

It was spring in South Dakota and winter had finally given way to it, albeit grudgingly. Flowers that had bloomed so profusely two months ago when Coralie left California were just now beginning to unfold their blossoms in her mother's carefully tended garden.

Pink peonies, purple and yellow irises, and golden daffodils provided a riot of color, as did the delicate cherry and crab apple blossoms that covered the trees like pink and white clouds. Life was peaceful for Coralie in Winner. Too peaceful. She had far too much time to think, to remember, to grieve.

Such as right now. She was supposedly weeding the backyard garden, but although she sat crosslegged on the ground, her hands were folded in her lap and her mind was far away in Idaho. Did Jim miss her? She knew Buck did. He'd written and told her so.

Jim wrote, too. He also telephoned, but she returned his letters unopened and refused his calls. It would have broken her heart to do that if that vital organ hadn't already been shattered by her departure from the farm that night.

That had been a heartbreaking experience. Buck had agreed to drive her to a motel in Copper Canyon, but on the way she talked him into taking her on to Lewiston that evening. She knew if she remained close by to Jim he'd talk her into staying, and that would only have postponed the inevitable. Their love was doomed, and the sooner she accepted that fact the less permanent damage there would be.

Or so she'd thought. Actually, the damage had already been done. She'd been thoroughly miserable since then. Oh, she'd had lots of support from her family. She'd cried in her mother's arms and told everyone the whole story, embarrassing though it was to admit she'd been stupid enough to answer an ad for a mail order bride.

Her parents, brother and sister, grandparents, aunts, uncles and cousins had all rallied around and tried to ease her suffering. They'd had parties for her, escorted her to local social events, introduced her to all their friends and even fixed her up with a couple of dates. She'd gone along, hoping all the activity would help, but nothing could dull the pain of a broken heart.

All the attention was beneficial in one way, though. It helped her to realize that healing had to come from within herself, and she started making plans to stop just existing and start living again.

One of her cousins lived and worked in Chicago, and she'd written to invite Coralie to come there and share her apartment while she looked for a job. It would put even more distance between Jim and herself, and she really needed to get back to work. But more important, it would give her something to occupy her mind and her empty time.

Besides, she'd been on "vacation" for two months and was getting dangerously low on money.

She'd gratefully accepted and was looking forward to catching a flight to O'Hare Field on the following Sunday.

Her reverie was broken by a voice calling to her. Coralie looked up and saw her mother coming across the yard. Laurel Dixon was a pretty woman, forty-six years old with brown hair cut short and turquoise eyes.

Coralie waved her arm. "Hi, Mom, I'm over here."

As Laurel drew closer Coralie could see the look of concern on her face. Hurriedly, she stood. "What's the matter, Mom?"

Laurel didn't waste words. "There's someone here to see you."

Coralie brushed the grass off her white shorts. "Oh. Who?"

"I think you'd better come and see for yourself," her mother said as the two of them headed for the house.

"Well, who is it, Mother?" Then a thought struck her. "Oh, no, it's not Harley again, is it? He's a nice enough guy, but he keeps pestering me to go out with him and I don't want to."

They went in through the back door and walked across the kitchen toward the living room.

"I've told him no several times, but—" She stopped when she saw her dad sitting on the couch talking to a teenage girl who was also seated and had her back to Coralie.

It took just a second for her to recognize the shoulder-length wavy brown hair, and the shock that bolted through her shook her to the very core.

"Gloria!"

Frantically, her gaze searched the room and found Jim standing alone in the corner by the piano.

It had to be a mirage! Or maybe she was hallucinating. She'd read that people who are deeply troubled sometimes do.

But Jim was no hallucination. He was much too vital and male.

Their gazes caught and held and everyone else faded away. She saw the suffering in his eyes, the dark shadows under them, and knew that she'd put them there.

Oh, darling, I wanted to make our parting easier for you, not more difficult.

He was wearing a brown tweed sport coat and matching brown slacks, and he was handsomer and sexier than any movie star. She ached to feel his arms around her, his mouth nibbling at hers.

Jim was hypnotized by Coralie's deep blue eyes that had grown dark with pain. He knew he was responsible.

Sweetheart, all I ever wanted was to love you and keep you with me. I never meant to hurt you.

She was wearing short white shorts and a sleeveless red shirt. He'd never seen her long shapely legs and her willowy arms bare before, but he wasn't surprised by her perfection. She'd always radiated sex appeal, even in jeans and a heavy sweatshirt. If only he could touch her, hold her...

He was the first to speak. "Coralie, I apologize for not telling you we were coming."

His voice sounded rusty, as if he hadn't used it in a long time, and he cleared his throat. "I talked by phone with your dad, but swore him to secrecy. I was certain that if you knew, you wouldn't see us, and what we have to say is vitally important."

Coralie's head was spinning, and she leaned against the wall to steady herself. "Wh-what are you doing here?"

"I came to plead with you to come back home with me," he said simply.

Come home with him? If only she could. "But you know I can't do that. Gloria..."

She turned toward the sofa and saw that her dad and Gloria were now standing, too. What was going on here?

Almost as if she'd read Coralie's thoughts Gloria said, "I came with Dad so I could apologize to you."

"Why?" Coralie hadn't meant to sound so abrupt, but she'd been shocked too far off center to be gracious.

The girl looked confused and hesitated. "Be-because Dad's been so sad, and quiet, and just plain miserable ever since you left. So has Grandpa, and Amber."

Coralie's eyes widened with surprise. She'd never expected Gloria to admit that. She looked at Jim, and he nodded his agreement.

She again turned her attention to Gloria. "And you? How have you felt about my leaving?"

Jim's daughter looked embarrassed. Or was she shy? "I was glad at first," she acknowledged, and was raised several notches in Coralie's esteem for telling the truth no matter how difficult.

Coralie's dad, Ivan, broke in. "If you'll excuse us your mother and I will leave you three alone to talk."

He and Laurel started to walk away, but Jim stopped them. "If you don't mind I'd like for you both to hear what Gloria and I have to say."

They nodded and returned, and Coralie was even more confused.

She returned her attention to Gloria. "Did...did something change your mind about me?" She wasn't going to let herself start to hope again.

"I didn't so much change my mind about you as about myself," Gloria said. "I always knew you were a nice person. That's why I felt so threatened by you."

She turned pink and looked away. "I...I was afraid Dad wouldn't...wouldn't love me anymore if he married you."

Coralie could feel the child's humiliation at confessing such a personal fear in front of everybody, and she wondered why Jim was permitting it.

She walked over to where Gloria stood, but didn't touch her. "Honey," she said softly, "your father will always love you. That's why I left. I was afraid he'd never love me as much as he does you.''

Her eyes widened. "You were? But I was being such a brat. Nobody could love me—''

A sob shook her, and Coralie couldn't hold back any longer. She reached out and took Jim's daughter in her arms. Gloria buried her face in Coralie's shoulder and started to cry.

Coralie comforted her with strokes and murmured assurances. "I was behaving so childishly that I was sure he could never love me," she confessed. "He already had two beautiful and cherished daughters, he didn't need another one. He needed a wife who was mature enough to be a helpmate, not a hindrance. I certainly didn't fit that description, so you see, honey, we were both at fault.''

She glanced at Jim, who was still standing at the piano looking a little stunned, and managed a soft chuckle. "It's a wonder he hasn't sworn off all women for good.''

Gloria chuckled, too, then raised her head and stepped out of Coralie's embrace. "I guess you're right. That must be why he and I started seeing a family counselor.''

That really startled Coralie. "You've been getting counseling?''

This time it was Jim who spoke. "Sam arranged for us to see a psychologist who works with the district family court. Her name is Marilyn Offenbach, and Gloria and I have been seeing her twice a week. She's helped us both tremendously. I guarantee you my parenting skills are a whole lot better now than they were.''

"Yeah," Gloria said in mock disgust. "Amber and I don't get away with half the things we used to. Our rooms haven't been so clean since Mo—''

She cut off the word and looked distressed.

Coralie came to her rescue. "Since your mother left," she finished for her. "Don't be afraid to mention your mother in front of me. It's natural that you should think about her, and I'd never have tried to take her place. I just hoped you, Amber and I could be good friends.''

Gloria smiled. ''I hope we can be, too, now. If you come back I can't promise to turn into an angel overnight. I'm pretty sure it will take a lot more counseling to accomplish that, but I will try to be more likable....''

Again Coralie put her arms around the girl and hugged her. ''You can never be more lovable than you are right now,'' she murmured huskily. ''Don't sell yourself short, honey, and if I come back I'll try to grow up and be more understanding.''

Gloria hugged her back. ''I guess neither of us can promise more than that.''

They broke apart, and Coralie looked around the room. Jim hadn't moved or said anything, but he looked hopeful, although still uncertain and fearful. Her parents were beaming. Obviously, they liked Jim and Gloria and would be happy to accept Jim's family into their own.

All this was very nice, but she and Jim still had to talk, and without any onlookers. She smiled and turned to her mother. ''Mom, would you and Dad take Gloria down to the Confectionary and introduce her to a Peanut Buster Supreme?''

The Confectionary was the local ice-cream parlor where the young people hung out, and a Peanut Buster Supreme was one of their extra-gooey specialties.

''I want to talk to Jim privately.'' She looked at Gloria. ''Do you mind?''

Gloria grinned. ''Of course not. That's what we came here for, and besides, I can't wait to find out what a Peanut Buster Supreme is.''

They left, and Coralie and Jim were finally alone. She looked at him and started to tremble. The width of the room between them seemed like an insurmountable distance. Was there really hope that they could spend the rest of their lives together, after all?

Well, every journey started with the first step. Jim had traveled across three states to see her, she should be able to come the last fifteen feet.

She took one step, then another. He started walking, too, and then they were in each other's arms. He was also trembling and it was only then that she realized the inner turmoil he was going through. "Coralie, my darling, how could you doubt my love for you?" he asked raggedly. "I've never been so miserable in my life as I have been these past weeks without you. What do I have to do to prove it?"

She raised her face to his and murmured, "Kiss me."

He lowered his head to cover her hungry mouth with his own. Their kiss was long, and ravenous, and insistent, and when they finally broke it off she was dizzy as well as shaky. He cradled her against him. "Now do you believe me?"

"How could I not?" Her voice was as ragged as his, and she put her open mouth against his neck and sucked gently.

He shivered, and she whispered in his ear, "Do you like that?"

"Oh, yes," he said hoarsely. "But if you give me a hickey how am I going to explain it to your parents?"

"No need," she assured him softly. "They know where hickey's come from."

"I'll bet they do at that," he said and kissed her again.

When they finally had to come up for air he sighed and nibbled on her earlobe. "Sweetheart, don't keep me in suspense," he begged. "Is there a chance in hell that you'll come back home and marry me? I've missed you so. I can't sleep at night, and wander around in a daze during the day. I don't think I can survive much longer without you. I swear things will be different."

She'd never realized that the ear was an erogenous zone, but he was sending tingles down her spine. "I've missed you, too," she admitted breathlessly. "I couldn't stop thinking about you, wanting you, needing you. Wondering if there was something I could have done differently to earn Gloria's approval.''

Coralie shivered in his arms as his tongue fondled her lobe. "Does she really mean what she said?" The words sort of ran together.

He kissed her lobe, then released it. "Yes, honey, she does. That's why I brought her here with me. She wanted to come and tell you herself that she's changed."

His palms roamed over her back, relaxing some muscles and tightening others. "The counseling sessions have helped us both to understand her possessiveness toward me. It's pretty much like you said—she's afraid I'll abandon her, too, and therefore she holds on too tight. She understands that now, and she really does want you to come back."

Coralie sighed. "I want to go back with you. I think I'd sell my soul for the privilege, but I don't want to cause trouble between you and your daughters."

His hands roamed lower over her derriere. "You won't," he assured her huskily. "Now that I've had some counseling I won't let that happen."

His voice dropped to a lower, sexier pitch. "Besides, what about those two sons you promised me? I'd really like to get started on them."

She pressed against him, reveling in his obvious arousal. "So would I," she assured him tenderly and brushed her lips across his. "We'd better set the wedding date for very soon."

"Yes, ma'am," he said with a sigh and captured her mouth with his own.

*   *   *   *   *

COMING NEXT MONTH

#1138 A FATHER FOR ALWAYS—Sandra Steffen
Fabulous Fathers
To keep his daughter, single dad Jace McCall needed a fake
fiancée—fast! So when he asked Garret Fletcher to be his pretend
bride, Garret couldn't refuse. After all, she didn't have to pretend
she was in love....

#1139 INSTANT MOMMY—Annette Broadrick
Daughters of Texas/Bundles of Joy
Widowed dad Deke Crandal knew horses and cattle—not newborn
baby girls! So how could Mollie O'Brien resist Deke's request for
help? Especially when she secretly wished to be a permanent part
of the family.

#1140 WANTED: WIFE—Stella Bagwell
Lucas Lowrimore was ready to settle down—with Miss Right. He
just didn't expect to fall for pretty police officer Jenny Prescott.
She was definitely the wife he wanted, but Jenny proved to be a
hard woman to win!

#1141 DEPUTY DADDY—Carla Cassidy
The Baker Brood
Carolyn Baker had to save her orphaned godchildren from their
uncle, Beau Randolf! What would a single farmer know about *twin*
infants? But Beau wasn't the greenhorn Carolyn had expected!

#1142 ALMOST MARRIED—Carol Grace
Laurie Clayton thought she'd never love again—until
Cooper Buckingham charmed her and the baby she was caring for.
Everything seemed perfect when they were together, almost as if
they were married! But would Laurie ever be able to take a chance
and say, "I do"?

#1143 THE GROOM WORE BLUE SUEDE SHOES—
Jessica Travis
With his sensuous sneer and bedroom eyes, Travor Steele was a
dead ringer for Elvis Presley. But it was gonna take a whole lotta
shakin' to convince Erin Weller that he wasn't the new king—but
her next groom!

Take 4 bestselling love stories FREE

Plus get a FREE surprise gift!

DEPUTY DADDY
by Carla Cassidy
Book one of her brand-new miniseries

Who should raise the orphaned twins?

"Me, their godfather. Just because I'm a man doesn't mean I can't warm up formula or read bedtime stories. Besides, I love those two little rascals."
—Beau Randolph

"Me, their godmother. Those kids need a stable, parental figure, and what could a carefree bachelor know about raising babies?
—Carolyn Baker

Look for *Deputy Daddy* in March.

The Baker Brood continues each month:

Mom in the Making in April (SR #1147)
An Impromptu Proposal in May (SR #1152)
Daddy on the Run in June (SR #1158)

only from

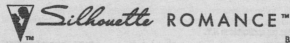

INTRODUCING...

A collection of award-winning books by award-winning authors! From Harlequin and Silhouette.

Heaven In Texas
by Curtiss Ann Matlock

National Reader's Choice Award Winner— Long Contemporary Romance

Let Curtiss Ann Matlock take you to a place called *Heaven In Texas*, where sexy cowboys in well-worn jeans are the answer to every woman's prayer!

"Curtiss Ann Matlock blends reality with romance to perfection!" —*Romantic Times*

Available this March wherever Silhouette books are sold.

As seen on TV!

Free Gift Offer

With a Free Gift proof-of-purchase from any Silhouette® book, you can receive a beautiful cubic zirconia pendant.

This gorgeous marquise-shaped stone is a genuine cubic zirconia—accented by an 18" gold tone necklace.

(Approximate retail value $19.95)

Send for yours today...
compliments of ▼ *Silhouette®*
TM

To receive your free gift, a cubic zirconia pendant, send us one original proof-of-purchase, photocopies not accepted, from the back of any Silhouette Romance™, Silhouette Desire®, Silhouette Special Edition®, Silhouette Intimate Moments® or Silhouette Shadows™ title available in February, March or April at your favorite retail outlet, together with the Free Gift Certificate, plus a check or money order for $1.75 u.s./$2.25 CAN. (do not send cash) to cover postage and handling, payable to Silhouette Free Gift Offer. We will send you the specified gift. Allow 6 to 8 weeks for delivery. Offer good until April 30, 1996 or while quantities last. Offer valid in the U.S. and Canada only.

Free Gift Certificate

Name: _____

Address: _____

City: _____ State/Province: _____ Zip/Postal Code: _____

Mail this certificate, one proof-of-purchase and a check or money order for postage and handling to: SILHOUETTE FREE GIFT OFFER 1996. In the U.S.: 3010 Walden Avenue, P.O. Box 9057, Buffalo NY 14269-9057. In Canada: P.O. Box 622, Fort Erie,

---

FREE GIFT OFFER
079-KBZ-R
ONE PROOF-OF-PURCHASE

To collect your fabulous FREE GIFT, a cubic zirconia pendant, you must include this original proof-of-purchase for each gift with the properly completed Free Gift Certificate.

079-KBZ-R

Welcome to the

A new series
by Carol Grace

This bed and breakfast offers great views, gracious hospitality—and possibly even love!

You've already met proprietors Mandy and Adam Gray in LONELY MILLIONAIRE (Jan. '95). Now this happily married pair invite you to stay and share the romantic stories of how two other very special couples found love at the Miramar Inn:

ALMOST A HUSBAND—Carrie Stephens needed a fiancé—fast! And her partner, Matt Graham, was only too happy to accommodate, but could he let Carrie go when their charade ended?

AVAILABLE SEPTEMBER 1995

ALMOST MARRIED—Laurie Clayton was eager to baby-sit her precocious goddaughter—but she hadn't counted on Cooper Buckingham playing "daddy"!

AVAILABLE MARCH 1996

Don't miss these charming stories coming soon from

♥ *Silhouette* ROMANCE™

MIRAM

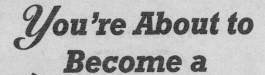